DREAMWORKS

PUSS IN BOOTS

THE NOVEL

WITHDRAWN

by Lara Bergen

BANTAM BOOKS

PUSS IN BOOTS: THE NOVEL
A BANTAM BOOK 978 0 857 51086 0

First published in Great Britain by Bantam, an imprint of Random House Children's Books
A Random House Group Company

This edition published 2011

10 9 8 7 6 5 4 3 2 1

The Random House Group Limited supports The Forest Stewardship Council (FSC®), the
leading international forest certification organisation. Our books carrying the FSC label are
printed on FSC® certified paper. FSC is the only forest certification scheme endorsed by
the leading environmental organisations, including Greenpeace. Our paper procurement
policy can be found at www.randomhouse.co.uk/environment

MIX
Paper from
responsible sources
FSC
www.fsc.org   FSC® C016897

Bantam Books are published by Random House Children's Books,
61–63 Uxbridge Road, London W5 5SA

www.totallyrandombooks.co.uk
www.kidsatrandomhouse.co.uk

Addresses for companies within The Random House Group Limited can be found at:
www.randomhouse.co.uk/offices.htm

THE RANDOM HOUSE GROUP Limited Reg. No. 954009

A CIP catalogue record for this book is available from the British Library

Printed and bound by CPI Group (UK) Ltd, Croydon, CR0 4YY

CHAPTER

ONE

Through the years, he had been known by many names: Diablo Gato, the Furry Lover, Chupacabra, Friskie Two-Times and, of course, the Ginger Hit Man. But to most, he was simply Puss In Boots . . . outlaw. To them, he was just another fugitive, forever running from the law, with no place to call home and no friends or family to turn to. But as he moved from town to town, slinking through the shadows, Puss never lost faith that one day he would find a way to clear his name. And then one fateful night, in the lonely, dusty town of Santa Maria Margarita de Juan Jose Julio, when Puss was least expecting it, his chance finally came . . .

1

It was the *Festival del Fuego y el Pollo* – or as the *gringos* called it, the Fire and the Chicken Festival – which meant great bonfires in the town square . . . and a guy in a chicken costume clucking his head off and running around. As the revellers whooped and hollered and shot off fireworks in the streets, the rougher folk in town were celebrating in their own way in the saloon. The poker tables were full and the bar was lined with thirsty *hombres*, while the piano player banged out cheerful tunes in hopes of keeping tempers cool. Before long, though, grim footsteps clicked along the wood-plank sidewalk, and the music died away as a long shadow stretched across the barroom floor. All eyes turned to the swinging doors . . . then travelled down to the tiny figure silhouetted beneath them.

"HA-HA!" Peals of laughter instantly broke the silence. A cat? In a hat? And *boots*! *Ay caramba!* How *loco* was that?!

"Here, kitty, kitty," jeered one bar patron as the cat strode coolly by him.

The stranger's soft orange fur bristled for a moment, but he firmly stayed his course. As he neared the bar, however, a thief named Luis chuckled and nudged his sleeping partner.

"Raoul. Look what the cat dragged in. Oh, wait, that *is* the cat," the burly man scoffed.

The other thief lifted his eyes wearily, then bolted straight up at the startling sight. Luis slapped his back, and they both nearly fell off their stools as they shared a gut-splitting belly laugh.

The cat, meanwhile, ignored them. *Humanos*, he thought. It was the same old story in every bar, it seemed, so he was used to it by now. He knew that their sneers and jeers would turn into bows of respect soon enough.

Lightly, he sprang onto an open barstool right next to Luis, before rising on his toes to see over the bar. "One *leche*, please," he told the bartender. Then he pulled a thin gold ring out of his boot and flipped it – *clink* – onto the bar top.

The bartender picked up the ring and frowned.

He bit it to make sure it was real. Yep, there were teeth marks. The man eyed the stranger. Was it stolen? (*Si*. Indeed.)

"What are you doing here, *senor*?" the bartender asked his furry customer. A grin began to stretch across his face. "Did you lose your ball of yarn?"

"Ha-ha!"

"Har-har!" The saloon shook as peals of laughter ricocheted throughout the room. Even the lights above the bar swayed back and forth and shook.

"Heh, heh. So funny," the cat dully muttered. As if he'd never heard *that* one before.

The bartender dabbed tears of laughter away and took a minute to enjoy his joke. Then he slipped the gold ring in his vest pocket and grinned. "One *leche* coming up."

As the bartender poured the cat's milk, however, Luis got a bitter gleam in his dark eye. He reached out and yanked the stool out from under the cat, who luckily grabbed the edge of the bar just in time. But *uh-oh* . . . as he dangled two feet off the ground by his claws, the cat's boots began to slip off. Finally, they fell to the floor with a *clunk*, and once again the crowd started to roar.

But this time, the sound was interrupted rather quickly by the *zeesh!* of a dagger flying across the room. It zoomed by several crooked noses, and nearly grazed a dozen scarred, stubbled chins, before it landed with a *thwack!* in the center of a tiny "Wanted" poster – the last in a long line of them.

The hunted outlaw was named Puss In Boots. WANTED FOR ROBBERY it said. Instantly, the bar went silent as the patrons recognized the pink-nosed face, and with looks full of dread they turned back toward the stranger . . . He was *him*!

By this time, Puss was seated at a table. His arms were folded across his chest. With a tip of his feathered hat he reassured them. "I am not looking for trouble," he said. "I am but a humble *gato* in search of his next meal." His golden eyes perused the stone-silent barroom. "Perhaps you gentlemen can help me find a simple score."

Raoul stood up, his eyes hard as steel and his frown crooked and mean. He ripped the wanted poster off the wall. "The only thing you'll find tonight is trouble, Puss In Boots," he declared.

Puss, however, smiled. As if an amateur robber could scare *him*. There was only one thing he was afraid of . . . then suddenly, he realized it was walking by right then! A policeman was passing just outside the saloon. Puss leaned back into the shadows and hid. He sighed when the footsteps of the law fell silent. *That was close,* he thought to himself.

Raoul's face, meanwhile, broke into a sinister grin. "Well, perhaps if *one* of us were to tell the law that you were in town . . ." he began. And as if on cue, Luis and a third thief, Giuseppe, got up and joined him. "We could split the reward," Raoul finished.

But before the thieves could grab Puss, there was a flash of gleaming steel. In an instant, the cat had disarmed the thieves and trimmed their moustaches *and* beards.

Smiling, Puss sat down, leaned back and crossed his tall black boots on the table in front of him. He settled the tip of his sword on Giuseppe's thick throat. "You made the cat angry. You do not want to make the cat angry," he hissed. Then – *zing!* – his claws sprang out like five needle-sharp switchblades. Giuseppe shook so hard at the sight of them, his trousers fell from his waist.

Puss sighed. He had made his point he decided, as he looked around the saloon again. *Now, let's try this once more,* his eyes told the wide-eyed crowd. Was there anyone who could help him find a place to rob that night?

"Uh . . . the Church of Saint Michael has just put up a golden statue of the Virgin of Guadalupe," suggested the bartender nervously.

But Puss immediately shook his head. "I do not steal from churches," he said, smoothing the yellow feather on his hat.

Another customer spoke up. "The Boys' Orphanage received a donation of silver candlesticks that would look very lovely in your home."

Puss frowned, irritated. "I do not steal from orphans," he declared.

Raoul, Luis and Giuseppe exchanged quick, furtive looks.

"What about Jack and Jill—" began Giuseppe.

"*Ssh!* Are you crazy?" Luis shook his head.

"The *what*?" Puss's eyes narrowed. He wanted to hear more about this "Jack and Jill".

Raoul glanced at the other thieves. *What choice do we have?* his eyes seemed to say. He shrugged and took a deep, defeated breath, then he reluctantly explained: "The murderous outlaws Jack and Jill have gotten their hands on magic beans."

Puss's eyes grew wide at the sound of the words, and his mouth grew hard and stern. "Do not joke with me about magic beans," he warned, aiming his sword at Raoul's throat this time. "I searched half my life for them. They do not exist."

Luis shook his head. "No, cat. We have seen them," he said.

Earnestly, Raoul nodded. "These are the beans of legend," he agreed. Then he raised his arm and revealed a bright blue tattoo on his wrist of just such a magic bean.

Puss's jaw fell open. *Could it be?* he wondered as his heart thumped beneath his ribs.

"Grows a vine to the Land of Giants and the Golden Goose," Luis went on explaining as Raoul unbuttoned his shirt. On Raoul's arm Puss could see a vine growing, eventually reaching a castle that covered his chest. From there, the vine ran up and over his shoulder, to a large yellow goose on the thief's hairy back.

"The Golden Goose," Puss said softly, staring. Ah, but he knew the story well . . .

"A heist like this could set you up for life," Raoul said with a smile that said he'd been thinking about it himself for some time.

"All *nine* of them," Luis joked and grinned. But Puss was clearly in no mood for laughs.

Luis cleared his throat and lowered his voice. "But only a cat with a death wish would steal the beans from Jack and Jill," he said.

At this, Puss rose to his feet on his chair and set his boot firmly on the worn tabletop. "The only wish I have is to repay an old debt. And this is my chance," he declared. Then he hopped down and planted both boots firmly on the stone floor. He rested his paws on the belt cinched around his furry hips. "Now, where do I find this Jack and Jill?"

CHAPTER
TWO

Meanwhile, a rickety old wagon pulled into town. It was drawn by a team of snorting, red-eyed, fiery-tempered hogs. And it was driven by a couple just as wild and mean – and far, far uglier.

The man was dressed in a suit of matted red velvet, two or three sizes too small for his pot-bellied frame. He wore a hat that was gray and floppy, and a wide lace collar that had once been white. (Countless drips from his hairy double chin, however, had stained it a rather repulsive shade of dingy brown.) The woman was just as wide as her husband and dressed in a moth-eaten blue waistcoat and mud-splattered skirt. Her greasy black hair was pulled back in a tight, slick bun, which unfortunately revealed her face. This included a narrow forehead with eyebrows that formed an arrow pointing straight down to her frown. She was Jill, and Jack was her husband, and yes, they did have magic beans – safe in a football-sized steel strong-box locked tight around Jack's meaty, clenched fist.

The wagon ground to a halt, finally, in front of the town's one hotel. Sourly, the couple clambered down and climbed the hotel steps. They each kicked a door open and the lobby fell silent as they walked in.

Jill sniffed and frowned, then grabbed the gun from Jack's belt and – *BANG!* – fired off a round.

Jack looked around. "What was it, Jill?"

"I don't think I got it," she said with a shrug.

Then a body dropped from the balcony above. She grinned. *Hmm?* Perhaps she was wrong!

By that time, the lobby was empty. The patrons had fled as fast as they could. Jack and

Jill were *not* a couple you wanted to be around if you had a choice. Alas, the hotel clerk was not so lucky and had to stay behind. He was huddled behind the front desk.

Jack and Jill stomped up and Jack pounded on the desk bell with his iron-clad fist.

Slowly, the clerk stood up, wincing. "Y-y-y-e-s?" he stammered at last.

Jack grinned, revealing crooked rows of yellowed teeth and a few empty gaps where they'd fallen out. After signing for their room, Jack announced, "We'd like a complimentary continental breakfast!"

Jill nodded and then struck a match using Jack's unshaven chin. "And don't even think about skimping on them baby muffins," she warned.

A little later, in their hotel room, Jill got ready to give Jack a much-needed shave. She pulled out the long, straight razor and carefully inspected the bright, shiny blade. Then she took the stiff leather strop and expertly rubbed the razor back and forth. To test if it was sharp enough, she yanked a greasy hair from Jack's head and sliced. Half fell lightly to the floor. *That'll do*, Jill thought to herself.

"You know, Jill, I've been thinking," Jack spoke up as Jill soaped his chin. He was about to bring up a delicate subject and he wasn't quite sure where to begin.

She frowned and waited impatiently. "Get it out," Jill finally snapped.

"I . . . um . . ." Jack twisted in his seat. "Uh . . . once we're done with this magic bean business and got ourselves all them beautiful golden eggs—"

"Mm-hm? Go on." Jill put down the soap brush and lifted Jack's chin. She set the cold steel blade against his neck and gazed down at him, waiting.

"That we cut down on some of the hijacking and murdering," Jack went on. "I mean, it's fun and all but . . . I want a baby."

Jill leaned in. "A baby what, Jack?"

"A baby *us*, Jill. Something we can dress up and feed."

A baby? Jill could feel her lunch starting to rise. The very thought made her shudder and want to throw up. "You *really* want to have this conversation when I'm holding this blade?" she asked, narrowing her eyes.

Jack shrugged and smiled at her hopefully and tried to appeal to her softer side: "It wouldn't hurt to have an extra shooter during ambushes."

At the same time, just outside their window, an orange cat – with boots – was perched on the sill. Puss peered in and saw the couple arguing . . . then his eyes landed on the box still locked around Jack's hand. The magic beans inside actually made it glow with an eerie greenish-blue light. "Holy *frijoles*," he gasped, amazed. They truly *did* exist after all!

While Jack and Jill continued debating the pros and cons of parenthood, Puss released his longest, sharpest claw and traced a line on the windowpane exactly his own shape and size. Then he used the pads of his paws to very carefully pop the silhouette out. Pleased with his work, he sighed and prepared to slip inside. But before he could, another small figure leaped up onto the other windowsill right next to his. It was a cat – that was obvious – all black except for the snow-white tip of his tail. His face was completely hidden, though, by a black leather mask.

Puss watched, stunned, as the masked stranger raised the window in front of him and briskly leaped inside.

"Hey! What gives?" Puss whispered angrily. The cat even had boots, just like him!

Lightly, the masked stranger sprinted across the room straight toward Jack. He was after the magic beans, too, Puss realized. "No! No! *No!*" Puss hissed, outraged, and he bounded in after him at once.

Silent but determined, Puss caught up to the masked thief. "You!" he whispered. "You! You stop where you are."

The stranger stopped and both cats peered

around the wall at the glowing box locked fast around Jack's hand.

Jill was still standing over Jack with the razor. "I don't know, Jack," they could hear her say. "How do I ride and shoot with a baby slung over my back?"

"They got them backpacks now," Jack told her. "The way I see it, Jill, we only fall off this flat earth one time."

The cats turned back to face each other. The stranger's eyes shone behind his mask.

"Those beans are mine!" Puss informed him.

But the stranger did not look impressed at all. In fact, the masked cat went on to make a gesture that very much resembled snapping Puss in half.

"You snap *me*?" Puss hissed, insulted.

The stranger nodded and did it again.

Puss narrowed his eyes and growled, but the stranger did the same. Puss had come this far. He was *not* backing down. But the stranger seemed to feel much the same way. They were locked in a standoff, standing there in their boots, glaring, face-to-face . . .

Then a loud *BOOM!* made them both suddenly jump back.

Puss looked down, surprised to see a hole blown clean through the floor between the stranger's boots and his. Then he looked up to see Jack and Jill's mean, ruddy faces staring down at them.

"You looking for something?" Jack sneered, wiping what soap was left, off his thick double chin.

"Heh, heh!" Jill cackled cruelly. She fixed a long, cold stare on them.

Puss turned to look at the masked stranger beside him only to find he wasn't there. Puss scanned the room and couldn't believe it: the cat was getting away and leaving him to face the thieves alone! As soon as the stranger reached the window, he leaped through and slammed it shut, trapping Puss inside. Slowly, Puss turned back and looked up at Jack and Jill.

"Uh, no. Housekeeping?" He shrugged. This line was lame, he knew, but it was worth a try, if only to stall for time while he decided what to do. Jack and Jill's faces darkened. They were clearly not amused.

Puss's only option was to escape – if he could. He turned and fled, springing through the Puss-shaped hole in the other window and landed in the street. Then – *ouch!* – a rock hit his head. He rubbed the sore spot and looked up to see the masked stranger holding another stone and rudely mocking him.

Puss made an angry fist. "You are going to pay for this!" he hissed.

At the same time – *bang!* – Jack leaned out the window and fired another shot at Puss from his gun. Puss ducked and took off down the street towards the stranger, who gracefully back-flipped away. Puss did a handspring of his own in response. Just who did that cat think he was anyway?

Puss followed the stranger around a corner

and watched him leap onto a low roof. He tried to slide away along a clothesline, but Puss slashed it with his dagger before he could. This sent the stranger back down into the street, but it didn't keep him from racing on. Puss followed along the rooftops, all the while keeping a sharp eye on him.

At last, Puss saw his chance to catch the masked stranger. He grabbed a rope and swung down, directly in the black cat's way.

"Ha-ha!" he cried victoriously . . . a split second before he missed the masked cat and slammed – hard – into a crate.

While Puss staggered back to his feet, groaning, the masked stranger continued on until he reached a dead end. Puss smiled. He had him for sure now! But then the stranger pulled one more trick. He dove through a cat-door-sized hole in the wall – and Puss dove straight in after him.

CHAPTER
THREE

Puss looked around. Where was he? Some kind of "cat cantina," it seemed. Dozens of round, green eyes stared back at him over earthenware dishes full of cream. Finally, his eyes landed on the masked stranger, who stood, tapping one boot, at the end of the bar. Puss strode toward him, his fur bristling furiously. His footsteps echoed as he marched.

"Those magic beans were *my* score!" Puss declared. "You just cost me a chance at getting the golden eggs, *mi amigo*. Put up your dukes!"

Puss balled his paws into fists and raised them, and the stranger raised his in return. Then suddenly a cat band in the background started playing, and instead of fighting, the stranger started to stomp his boots and wiggle his hips. Puss stood there, baffled, as the stranger flamencoed around him in fiery circles, then finally stopped. *Your turn,* he seemed to say then with a nod, while the other cats broke into applause.

Puss twitched his whiskers. *Huh?* What exactly was going on? Then he noticed a poster behind the bar. It said: TUESDAY NIGHT DANCE FIGHT — FREE ADMISSION. *Aha . . .*

"Very well," said Puss, pulling his boots up to their full, glorious height. "If it is to be a dance fight, then I will Tuesday-Night-Dance-Fight you to the *death!*" He waited for the music to start, then he raised his arms high, and soon his boots began to fly.

Finally, he finished with a dramatic flourish and froze, waiting for the crowd to cheer. The only sound he heard, however, was the slow clap of one pair of paws. Puss turned. It was coming from the masked stranger himself . . . as he balanced between two barrels in a full, impressive split. The cat clapped once more, then leaped down and kicked the dance fight into a whole new, much higher, gear.

As Puss watched, the stranger turned his back to him and began to kick his hind feet.

Puss cringed, appalled at the rude gesture. "How dare you do the Litter Box at me!"

But two could play at that game, Puss decided. He raised his tail and sat down and began to scoot across the floor. "Hello?" he called to the masked stranger. *Just try to top "the Worms"!* he thought.

The duel went on as the two cats continued to match each other move for move.

"Can you feel me?" taunted Puss.

The stranger hissed in reply, his own boots speeding up faster and faster, until they were practically on fire. Then all of a sudden, they kicked a milk dish accidentally . . . and a drop of milk hit Puss's boot.

"*Aaah!*" the cats in the cantina gasped as Puss furiously whipped out his sword.

"Fear me if you dare!" he growled. Nobody soiled his boots and lived!

The masked stranger drew his sword as well, and the blades met with a spine-tingling *CLANG!* And in this battle, too, the cats were perfectly matched. Then somehow, someway, Puss felt his own sword suddenly swatted out of his hand, and the next thing he knew, the point of the masked cat's sword was poking into his silky chest fur.

The stranger's blue eyes smiled behind his mask as he paused to bask in the thrill of his victory. Then – *whack!* – the sword fell out of his hand as Puss grabbed a guitar and slammed it into the stranger's face.

"*Oh!*" The stranger howled and clutched his mask. He turned to Puss, outraged, and tore it off. Only then did Puss realize that his opponent wasn't a *he* at all. It was, in fact, a *girl!*

She scowled at Puss indignantly. "You hit me on the head with a *guitar?*" Then she turned on the heel of her cuffed leather boot and stormed off in disgust.

"You are a *woman*?" said Puss, in disbelief.

The cantina crowd, too, was in shock.

"*Whoa,*" Puss winced. He wasn't sure which was worse: slamming a guitar in a girl's face or nearly losing a duel to her. On the other hand, she was, he realized, *muy* beautiful!

"Amateur," muttered the stranger as she sheathed her sword and left the bar.

"Wow," Puss purred. "*Senorita,* wait! Let me buy you some *leche*! I am a lover, not a fighter," he quickly called, chasing after her.

Eagerly, he followed her through a set of curtains into a dark and rather menacing back room. He looked around, hoping to see her somewhere, but oddly he seemed to be alone.

"Hello? You are hiding from me?" He grinned. "I like to play games too. I sense in you a kindred spirit." Then he paused and sniffed. "I smell something familiar," he said, his eyes narrowing, and he cautiously sniffed again.

"Something dangerous." He reached for his sword. "Something *breakfasty*."

At that moment, Puss's heart filled with dread and skipped a beat. *No!* he thought. Not that rotten egg. Not *him*!

"It's been a long time, brother," said a voice behind him.

"*Maldito huevo*," Puss groaned as he whipped out his sword and whirled around to face his egg-shaped best friend from childhood – and his enemy since then. "Humpty Alexander Dumpty," he said hotly. "How dare you show your face to me!"

The figure, who was almost all face, nodded understandingly. "I know you are angry. You have every right. But it is good to see you, Puss." He smiled a friendly smile and straightened the tiny hat on his pointy bald head. "Are those new boots?" he asked, looking down.

"No! They are the same boots I wore when you betrayed me!" Puss spat. His eyes narrowed until they were steely amber slits.

"Betrayed *you*?" Humpty argued. His smooth,

pale cheeks flushed red. "You left me cracked in pieces on a bridge, surrounded by soldiers. They wrote a song about it!"

"And how did we get on that bridge in the first place?" Puss asked, tapping his boot.

"Because we were brothers, and brothers are supposed to look after each other, not—"

"Humpty! Remember why we are here," called a firm voice from above.

The egg shut his mouth and Puss looked up to see the mysterious stranger, high in the rafters, gracefully jump down. She took her place by Humpty's side and Puss shook his head in disgust.

"I should have known. I had the magic beans in my grasp and you sent this very attractive devil woman to interfere! You are a curse on my life!" He gave Humpty a long, hard look. Then he turned his back on both of them.

"Whoa, whoa!" Humpty called as he waddled after Puss on spindly, stockinged legs. "Wait! Hear me out! OK, yes, yes, I sent Kitty to bring you here. But she is no ordinary thief."

Puss stopped and spun around. What *was* Humpty talking about? The stranger, meanwhile, lifted her chin. Then she slipped off a glove to reveal a dainty white paw underneath.

Humpty grinned. "She's Kitty Softpaws. The softest touch in Spain."

Puss frowned. He was not at all familiar – or impressed – by such a name. Then he realized that the black cat had *his* boots in *her* paws!

"That's a lot of heel for a guy, don't you think?" she said with a wink.

Puss looked down. His feet were *naked*! Kitty tossed his boots back to him and smiled.

Humpty went on, his pale face full of hope . . . and something else that Puss couldn't quite name. "Look, with Kitty's skill, your sword and my brain, we've got a fighting chance here. Come on, you of all people know that nobody's ever ripped off the Giant's castle and lived to tell the tale. You want to survive? You need a plan." Then the egg took from his pocket a well-worn journal that Puss recognized at once. Humpty opened it up to a page full of equations and detailed diagrams. "I've studied this job my whole life. You know that."

Puss sighed. Indeed, he did.

"Let's be honest. Without me, you don't even know where to plant the beans, Puss," Humpty said. "But Jack and Jill do. They're on their way."

Puss flicked his tail at the thought of the couple. The egg had a point, though it was hard to admit.

"We go up the beanstalk outlaws and we come down legends. So, what do you say?" The egg held out his hand. "Partners?" he asked Puss, grinning.

Puss studied the egg's hand for a second. *Wait! What am I thinking?* he suddenly asked himself. How many times had the egg betrayed him? How many times had he let Puss down? "No. Never again," he told Humpty, at last, spinning around and walking away.

But Humpty wasn't ready to give up yet. He scrambled to catch up to Puss. "I'm sorry, OK?"

he told him. "How long are you going to hold a grudge? It's been seven years." He did the math in his head. "That's like thirty-five cat years! You need me! And I need you."

By then, though, Puss was through the curtain and back out in the bar. There was nothing Humpty could say to him now that would ever change his mind.

"Puss! Do you have any idea what they do to eggs in San Ricardo prison? I'll tell you this, my friend: it ain't over easy," Humpty called.

Ugh. Puss flinched. He knew he shouldn't feel for guilty for helping send Humpty to prison all those years ago. And yet, he couldn't help it, no matter how far behind them it was or how hard he tried . . .

"*Adios,* Humpty Dumpty," he said finally, sighing, and he left the cantina without looking back. His heart, though, was much heavier now . . . and his mind was filled with doubt.

Meanwhile, back in the cantina, Humpty hung his huge, egg-shaped head. "Oh, this is bad, this is bad," he moaned.

"Don't worry, I'll take care of it," said Kitty. "I know how to speak 'meow'." She winked at Humpty and his face lit up as he watched her follow Puss into the night.

"You're terrific! You're my ace in the hole! Don't botch it!" Humpty called.

CHAPTER
FOUR

In the alley outside the cat cantina, Puss muttered bitterly under his breath: "... sad story with your twisted lies in your greasy shell that smells like old ham! I should crack you open for—" *Huh?* Puss stopped as a dot of light on the ground caught the corner of his eye. It moved ... and he followed it ... across the alley ... almost forgetting everything else.

"Look what I found!"

Puss looked up, startled, to see Kitty perched on a windowsill. In her paw was a bright coin – the source of the bouncing spot of light.

Kitty grinned and waved it at him. "Someone

forgot his money," she purred.

Puss frowned. It was *his* coin, he could see. Obviously she had stolen it, too.

"Oh, you are dangerous," he said, disgusted . . . and yet, he couldn't seem to look away. She was like no other cat he'd ever known . . . and he had known many.

Kitty jumped down to the street. She batted her lashes and slowly slinked by. "Humpty says you like danger. Just think of all the trouble we can get into. The two of us together? We can steal a lot of golden eggs." She smirked as she swiped Puss's hat, unnoticed. "And you owe me," she said.

Puss finally realized his head was hatless, and he snatched it back from her with a frown. "I *owe* you?" he asked, rolling his eyes. Exactly how?

"*Mm-hm.*" She nodded smartly. "You hit me in the head with a guitar."

Ah . . . Puss sighed apologetically. "I regret the guitar."

"OK," Kitty answered brightly. "I forgive you. So, you're in?"

Puss shook his head. "There is one teeny, tiny, itty-bitty problem."

"And what is that?" she asked

Anger clouded his golden eyes. "You work for the egg."

"Oh, come on, Puss," said Kitty. "What happened between you and Humpty that was so bad?"

Puss sighed again and his shoulders sank as if the whole world had fallen on them. "I am afraid that with me and Humpty, the scars are too deep," he softly answered.

Then he turned away and raised his paw to his forehead as a flood of painful memories came rushing over him. He bit his lip and looked down at his reflection in a muddy puddle. Woefully, it gazed back.

"It all started a long time ago . . ."

"Oh no." Kitty quickly raised her paws. "You really don't have to tell me your whole life story, *please*."

Puss turned and gently guided her to a crate.

"You may want to sit. It is, at times, quite painful," he warned, as he helped her take a seat.

"OK, here we go," Kitty muttered. She let her head fall into her paws.

Puss, meanwhile, took a long, deep breath. It was a story that had to be told . . .

"It was a year in which the rain had not fallen . . ." Puss began.

Back then, he was but a tiny kitten, without a family or a home – just a small woven basket in which he rode, curled up, while the prairie winds carried it along.

At last, the basket came to rest in a small, particularly dusty, little town, at a home for lost children where a kind, motherly woman named Imelda was in charge. Warmly she took the kitten Puss into her heart and raised him, along with forty more orphans, as if he were her own.

Little Puss was very shy then, though, far from the swashbuckler he grew up to be. He was all too easily bullied, and had no experience at making friends. But one orphan reached out to him at supper the very first night that he arrived . . . (Actually, he reached out to take Puss's plate of beans, but he also smiled and introduced himself).

"Humpty Alexander Dumpty," he said.

Puss stared back at him, wide-eyed, for he had never before seen a real, live, talking egg. (He was also a little put off by the smell, but he would soon get used to that).

Then suddenly, a freckled fist slammed down on the table right in front of Puss, causing him to jump.

"Hey, Whiskers!" the boy attached to the fist barked. "You're sittin' in Little Boy Blue's chair."

Another bully, standing next to the first one, grabbed Puss and lifted him up by the scruff of the neck.

"Aw, come on. Is this necessary?" Humpty spoke up bravely. "Why don't you pick on somebody your own size?"

"Who asked you, Breakfast?" spat the third, smallest – and meanest – boy. This was Little Boy Blue. He grabbed Humpty gruffly by the collar and dangled him high above the floor.

Humpty tried to smile and reason with him. "Remember what Imelda says, Boy Blue: if you're going to blow your top, you blow your horn instead, right?"

But Boy Blue just laughed and took the egg's hat and tossed it across the room. Then he cut his eyes eagerly to his two friends. "Let's spin him!" he jeered.

Humpty waved his arms as Boy Blue tossed him onto his back and he started to whirl. "Please don't spin me! Do not spin me! You don't want to see an egg throw up! No, no, no!" he begged.

But it was no use. The boys pointed and laughed, while Puss helplessly watched the spinning egg turn green. Finally, Puss realized he couldn't just stand there. He had to do something. Sure, the egg had taken the beans from his plate, but he had also stood up for him. From then on,

Puss decided, he would have Humpty Dumpty's back, just as Humpty had had his.

Puss suddenly sprang into action, leaping high in the air. He came down on a spoon, which sent it flying, end over end. Puss reached out and caught it and bounded up Boy Blue's back, raised the spoon and thwacked him on the head. Boy Blue fell to the floor like a sack of flour and his friends began to flee. But Puss quickly decided the bullies weren't getting off so easily. With a flick of his wrist, he took them *all* down with his trusty spoon and grinned.

"Wow." Humpty stood up, dizzy. He looked at the fluffy kitten and the pile of bullies, stunned. "That was very impressive. Thanks," he told Puss.

From then on, Puss kept his eye out for the strange, wobbly egg. There was something . . . *egg*-ceptional and intriguing about him, Puss had to admit.

The next day, Puss saw Humpty waddle out into a small shack in the corner of the yard. Curious, Puss followed him in and watched him plant three beans. Then Humpty turned on a contraption that precisely watered the soil . . . and Puss slowly inched closer to see how it worked.

"Oh, it's you," Humpty gasped, jumping and turning, surprised that he wasn't alone. He caught his breath and looked down, self-consciously, at his row of young plants. "I've been collecting for months now," he explained. "You never know when you're gonna get lucky. Know what I mean?" Humpty chuckled a little nervously. "Magic beans . . . is what they are."

Puss simply stood and stared at him. He had no idea on earth what the egg was talking about.

"Hello?" Suddenly the egg seemed worried. "You're gonna tell the other kids that I believe in magic now. Is that what you're gonna do?"

Puss looked from the egg to the plants and back, then he silently shook his head, *No*.

"No?" Humpty looked doubtful at first, but slowly a smile stretched across his smooth face. He was starting to realize that this kitten was different from the other kids at the orphanage.

"What's your name?" he asked.

Puss meowed in reply.

"Don't say much, do you?" Humpty rubbed his bump of a chin. "Well, I think I'll call you Puss," he said. And from that moment on, the two were best friends.

Puss soon discovered how very full Humpty's mind was of invention and determination to fulfill his dream. A day never went by, in fact, that the egg didn't talk about it.

"Oh, when I find those magic beans, they'll grow a vine straight up into the clouds where a terrible and a fearsome giant hoards his greatest treasure: the *Golden Goose*. Just one – just *one* – of her golden eggs could set me up for life! It's my destiny, Puss. I can't really explain it," he'd go on as he gazed up at the clouds, "but I just feel like I belong up there." It was if he'd been laid for that one single purpose and nothing more.

Puss still wasn't sure what the egg was talking about, but he was sure he wanted to be part of it. Humpty took his beans very seriously, however.

It took some time before he was completely comfortable sharing his dream with his new friend. "I don't want any dead weight holding me down," he told Puss.

Desperate, Puss responded with his saddest, most pleading face. His eyes were round as saucers and somehow at least twice as big.

"What are you doing? Oh, man, that's good," said Humpty, slightly unnerved. "The eye thing that you are doing, that is really splendid. OK, let me just think for a second." But there was really no denying such a pitiful face. "OK, uh, this is crazy, but I am considering a partnership. I just need to know one thing: can you commit?"

Puss blinked, and his eyes returned to normal. "*Si,* I can commit," he declared. They were the first words ever from Puss's lips.

"Oh, you can talk!" Humpty remarked.

And so the "Bean Club" was established.

"First rule of Bean Club: you do not talk about Bean Club," Humpty pronounced. "Second rule of Bean Club is: you don't talk about Bean Club."

Then the egg held out his finger. "You ready?" he asked Puss.

Puss nodded back. "Ready," he said, raising his own paw up.

Solemnly, Humpty took a needle-sharp pin and pricked his fingertip. A drop of lemony yolk oozed out. Then Humpty passed the pin to Puss, who pricked his paw as well. Finally, they clasped hands and together recited these sacred vows:

From this day forth, it shall be known,
never alone, always together,
Humpty and Puss, brothers forever.

CHAPTER
FIVE

As they got older, Puss and Humpty continued their quest for the Golden Goose and became quite a team. Humpty was the brains, for the most part, and Puss provided the skill, and together they devised the most elaborate schemes for getting beans, which meant nearly everything to them. And yet it seemed no matter how many clever gizmos Humpty invented, or how many beans they actually found, the pair never actually got any closer to reaching the clouds.

In fact, as the years passed, the quest for magic beans seemed more and more like the dreams of a child. At the same time, Humpty and

Puss began looking for trouble, and more often than not, that's just what they found. Humpty's plans for acquiring beans became less ethical, though they usually worked. However, the police became quite good at catching them and hauling them back to the orphanage in shame.

"Third time this month, Imelda. Next time it's jail time," the Comandante of the local police warned their foster mother one day. He had just nabbed Humpty and Puss for picking pockets in town . . . again.

"They're just kids," Imelda tried to tell him as she gave them each a sound smack on the back of the head.

"Ow!" they howled together.

But the policeman was tired of this excuse. "They are thieves," he declared.

"You are better than this," Imelda told Puss later. She'd started to give up on the egg, but not him. "I believe in you with all of my heart. Please do not let me down," she begged.

And Puss promised that he would not. A life

of crime was not, he knew, the kind of life he wanted to lead, though he still wished there was some way to help his friend Humpty fulfill his dream.

Of course, Puss knew that it would be hard to tell Humpty that he was done leading a life of crime. When it came to finding magic beans, the egg seemed willing to do anything at all. The next day, perched on a rooftop, Puss tried to think of what to say . . .

"Are you all right?" Humpty looked over at him, then mindlessly chucked a stone down into the street. "You're down, I get it. I hate this place. I cannot wait for us to get out of here," he said. "Throw a rock. It'll make you feel better." And he tossed another one bitterly to demonstrate. Instead of bouncing along the street, however, this one pinged off the back of a wagon, breaking the lock on the door . . . and the next thing they knew, the wagon door swung open and out burst an enormous, angry, snorting bull!

"Oh boy!" Humpty exclaimed as the bull took

off, charging down the street. The animal was completely out of control – and worse, he was headed straight towards an old woman hobbling along with a cane!

Humpty winced. "We should go," he said quickly.

But all Puss could think was, *Somehow, I must help!* Instinctively, he sprang into action and grabbed a clothesline and, with a sweep of his claw, slashed it and swung down to the street. Landing on all four paws on the bull's back, he firmly dug his claws in. The sudden sharp pain made the bull stop dead in his tracks, an inch at the most before he mowed the poor old woman down.

Almost immediately, stunned, grateful townspeople began to gather around Puss and cheer.

"He saved the Comandante's mother!" they cried, and the word rapidly spread like wildfire throughout the little town.

Soon the Comandante himself appeared. "You saved my mother!" he gushed. There was no way he could possibly ever thank the brave cat enough for his truly heroic deed. The least he could do, the police chief decided, was hold a ceremony to honour him.

And so the next day, the whole village gathered in the town square to watch the Comandante hang a big, bright medal in the center of Puss's furry chest.

"*Senor* Puss, he is a hero!" the Comandante announced to the cheering crowd. "Today we see that courage and bravery comes in all sizes."

Imelda climbed onto the podium then with an ornately carved box. "These are for you, my boy," she said as she raised the fancy lid. Puss peered in. Inside was a small feathered hat, a gleaming sword and an exquisite pair of tall leather boots. They were not quite large enough for a man to wear, but just the right size for a full-grown, devilishly-handsome orange cat. "Wear them as a symbol of honour and justice," said Imelda as Puss took them out and slipped them on.

Puss's heart nearly burst, and he was so

choked up, he could hardly speak. "I will make you proud, Mama," he humbly told her.

She wrapped her arms around him. "You already have, my Puss In Boots."

It was strange, some surely thought, to give a cat boots, and yet . . . no one could deny that he looked very, very good.

And that name: *Puss In Boots* . . . It was the name he'd longed for all his life! At last, he felt like *someone*, and not just an orphan anymore. Only one thing could have made Puss happier: to have shared such a special moment with his best friend. But Humpty stayed away from the square that day and began to avoid Puss from then on. And as the light of Puss's path grew brighter, Humpty's path grew far darker.

Within a week, in fact, Humpty was in prison, and Puss was bitterly bailing him out.

"*Gracias*, Comandante," Puss told the policeman as he unlocked the door to Humpty's cell.

"You're welcome." The Comandante nodded to Puss. He now had the utmost respect for the heroic young cat. But he was more distrustful than ever of the village's bad egg.

Humpty offered his hand to the policeman and gave him a fake, sunny grin. "Officer, I just want to thank you so very much. How's your mom?"

The Comandante wrinkled his nose in obvious disgust. "Be careful of the company you keep," he sternly warned Puss.

As soon as they were out of the jailhouse, Puss stepped up his pace. His shiny new boots clicked angrily across the hard, dusty street. He had told the egg again and again to stay out of trouble, but Humpty just wouldn't listen to him. Puss had already decided on the way to bail out Humpty that this would be the last time he cleaned up the egg's sticky mess.

"I know, I know," Humpty said, waddling after him. "Never should've tried something without you."

Puss stopped and pushed his hat back. Humpty just didn't get it! He shook his head. Puss was *done* with a life of crime . . . and him.

"You're not stealing lollipops anymore, Humpty. This is getting serious," he snapped.

"You're right." Humpty nodded. "We have to be smarter about this. Here, look." He smiled and pulled a set of plans out of his pocket and giddily unfolded it. "We need to think bigger. I've been casing the silversmith and it's perfect, you and me, in and out, fifty seconds tops!" he said.

Puss batted the plans away with his paws, utterly appalled. "Would you put that away?" he snapped. He looked around quickly to make sure no one was watching them. "This is our *home*," he tried to tell Humpty. "These people have done nothing to us!"

"Our *home*?" Humpty scoffed. "OK, I get it now. You get some fancy boots and now you're too good for me?"

"That is not true," Puss replied.

"Look, we weren't born here," Humpty reminded him. "We're orphans, and all we've got is each other." He arched one thin eyebrow. "You understand?"

Puss grimaced. Oh, he understood. He understood that Humpty would never learn! He grabbed the plans out of Humpty's hands and bitterly tore them in two. Being thieves was *not* the answer. "We are better than this," he huffed.

"But we're partners," Humpty said, wounded. He looked in dismay at the ripped plans at his feet.

"We are brothers," Puss said solemnly, "but I am not stealing anymore."

Humpty would not give up so easily, however, and within the week Puss was awakened in the middle of the night by one of his boots. As soon as it – *thump!* – hit his face, his eyes popped open to see Humpty, pale and trembling, standing over him in the moonlight.

"I'm in trouble, Puss," Humpty whispered.

"What has happened?" Puss asked.

"It's Boy Blue and his gang. I owe them some money."

Puss sighed and shook his head. More trouble. When would the egg ever learn? Part of him wanted to go back to sleep and let Humpty clean up this new mess alone. But he also knew the fragile egg was no match for Little Boy Blue. If the thug got his hands on Humpty, he'd scramble him good.

Besides, getting Humpty out of hot water wasn't a crime, it was just helping a friend. And so Puss got up and pulled on his boots and followed Humpty outside.

They crept through the empty streets until they reached a cart next to a large stucco building, and Humpty stopped. He looked nervously over his shoulder. "They're coming for me," he told Puss. "Just get me over this wall. I'll be right back."

Puss obliged the egg and gave him a boost, and Humpty disappeared behind the wall. Alone then, Puss scanned the moonlit street for any sign of Boy Blue. But the night, thankfully, was still . . . until Humpty's voice suddenly called out again: "We gotta go. Help me up the wall, get me up the wall. Hurry! Hurry!" he yelled.

Puss leaped up and reached out to help his friend, and that's when he saw the sign: SAN RICARDO BANK.

No! It can't be! Puss thought. *This was a heist!*

The next thing he knew – *wham!* – a bag full of gold sailed over the wall and into the back of the cart. Then another . . . and another. *B-r-r-r-ingggg!* rang the bank alarm.

"I got everything. We did it. Come on! Let's go!" Humpty cried. He hopped down and into the cart. At the same, a whole regiment of guards began to pour into the street.

Puss jumped into the cart after Humpty and stared at the egg in disbelief. "Humpty!" he cried. "How could you do this to me?"

"What are you talking about? I did you a favour. We can finally get out of here!" Humpty said with a generous grin.

Puss could feel the rage rising up from his boots. "This is all the money of the people. This is all they have," he told the egg. At the same time, his mind was reeling. He was furious with Humpty *and* himself. How could he have let Humpty trick him like this? And how was he going to get him to give the gold back?

Just then Puss felt something grab him from behind, and he spun around, still enraged, claws outstretched. Only then did Puss realize that it was the Comandante. Oh no! He'd made a terrible mistake! He cringed as the stunned commander lowered his hand to reveal a nasty slash across his face.

"You disgrace those boots!" the policeman barked at Puss.

"Comandante, please, I can explain!"

But the Comandante's eyes were unforgiving. He turned to the soldiers who had gathered around. "Arrest them!" He pointed to Humpty and Puss.

No! Puss panicked and almost without thinking he cracked the reins and the cart took off.

Beside him, Humpty beamed. "Hurry up! Get to the bridge!" he cried.

Puss turned to him, glaring. "You tricked me!" he yelled back.

"I had to," Humpty told him. "You left me no choice!"

Their cart, meanwhile, thundered down the cobblestone streets, past the town square, toward the bridge out of town. Behind them, the police followed on horseback, determined to chase them down. The commotion soon brought out the townsfolk, including the orphans and Imelda, none of whom could believe their eyes.

"Mama . . . " Puss's eyes met Imelda's.

"Pequeño." She stared back at him, heartbroken, as the cart full of gold flew by.

Filled with shame, Puss hung his head as the cart headed onto the bridge.

"Watch out!" Humpty cried suddenly.

But it was too late. The wagon swerved and drifted into the first bridge tower, ejecting Puss and Humpty from their seats.

"Oh no," Puss moaned as the cart flew over the side of the bridge, along with the gold. He ran to the railing and watched it all sink into the rushing river below.

Back on the bridge, dazed, Humpty called to him. "Puss, I can't get up. Puss! Help me, I can't get up."

Puss turned to see the egg on his back, wildly waving his feet and arms.

"Freeze!" Just then the Comandante appeared, charging toward them with the rest of his troops.

"Puss, save me!" Humpty wheezed helplessly.

Puss glanced from the soldiers to Humpty, then he finally shook his head. "Save yourself," he told Humpty, his face just as stony as the bridge. And with that, he climbed onto the railing, took a deep breath, and dove into the river.

CHAPTER

SIX

Puss had come to the end of his story. Kitty, to her surprise, was still awake.

"I lost everything I cared about that day," Puss said at last, with a heavy sigh. "My brother. My honour. And my home. All I thought about was the disappointment in my mama's eyes. And I have been running ever since."

Kitty nodded sympathetically. She could see how painful the past was. But wasn't that all behind him now? Wasn't it, finally, time to move on?

"The egg betrayed me," Puss said bitterly. "His lies cost me everything!"

"I see," said Kitty, moving closer. "But when

we get those golden eggs, Ginger, you'll pay back the town and get back everything you lost."

"You think *I* don't want to fix the past?" a third voice suddenly spoke up. The cats turned to see Humpty standing in the alley on a small tower of crates. He took a step forward, then stopped. "Uh . . . I can't get down," he said.

Kitty walked over and lifted him to the ground, and Humpty waddled up to Puss. "Listen," he said, his shell the very picture of remorse, "a day doesn't go by that I don't think about what I lost. I lost my best friend. My only friend."

Puss glowered and stalked away. Didn't the egg understand that the two of them were through?

But Humpty wasn't giving up. He waddled after Puss once more. "And I get it now, trust me. I got greedy and desperate and I let you down. I let myself down. All I'm asking for, Puss, is a second chance. Give me that second chance and I'll help you pay back San Ricardo. Please, Puss, let me show you what our friendship meant to me."

Puss sighed and wrung his paws. He had given the egg a second chance before. And a third. And a fourth. And every time Humpty had let him down. Puss wasn't giving him any more.

And yet . . . maybe Humpty had changed this time. Maybe he did deserve one more chance. And maybe this was just the chance Puss needed to clear his name and pay back his mama and the villagers of San Ricardo . . .

He weighed his choices in his mind, and then he finally turned around. "I will do it," he told Humpty.

"That's great!" Humpty's face broke instantly into a wide, sunny smile.

"I will do this for my mother and for San Ricardo, not for you," Puss declared. He stared down his pink nose at Humpty, his paw on the hilt of his sword. He wanted to make one thing perfectly clear: "We are not partners, and we are not friends!" he swore.

"OK," Humpty replied, nodding eagerly. "I promise this time I will not let you down. Yes!"

He pumped his fist. "I think we got our Bean Club back!"

The next few days were devoted to planning. Humpty had all the details already worked out. He was pretty sure that Jack and Jill were headed to a place called Dead Man's Pass. And so the team of three made their way there and took their places on opposite sides of a deep crevasse.

Humpty waited on one ledge, while Puss and Kitty hid on the canyon's other rim. And before long, just as Humpty predicted, a trail of dust appeared in the distance. Sure enough, it was Jack and Jill's wagon.

"This had better work," Puss muttered to Kitty as it neared.

"You just need to worry about your part," she replied, pulling her black mask over her head.

He looked at her.

"What?" she asked.

"Again with the mask?"

Puss could see her roll her ice-blue eyes as she coolly fixed her gloves.

"I don't need style advice from Mr. Dusty Boots," she told him, nodding toward his feet.

Huh? Puss looked down, then back up, as Kitty launched herself effortlessly off the ledge.

Her timing was perfect. She bounded into the canyon just as the wagon rolled up, and with one graceful leap she landed smoothly on the top. Puss, meanwhile, ran along the ledge awkwardly before he finally decided to jump. But instead of landing on top of the wagon, he went sliding off the front. For a second, he dangled just behind Jack and Jill's head, and they would surely have seen him if they'd turned around, but fortunately they were *still* debating baby stuff.

"Our biological clocks are tickin', darling," Jack was telling Jill. "You've got to start lookin' at the big picture."

"Why don't we start with a hamster," said Jill. "Oh, we can't do that, can we, Jack? Remember what happened last time to Hamlet? You sat on it, Jack. And I had to bury it. I don't think so. We're going to start small. Just *pretend* you have a baby."

While they argued, Kitty grabbed Puss's tail and pulled him up next to her. Then she leaned over to open the wagon door. They could see the glowing box locked around Jack's hand. As planned, Puss held on tightly to Kitty's feet as she dove down and reached in for it.

"Hey, hey, hey!" Puss whispered.

"What?" asked Kitty.

"Look!" Puss nodded toward a whole litter of piglets just below the box. They were the same kind of wild, red-eyed hogs that were pulling the wagon, but luckily they were still babies and all still asleep.

Kitty realized she'd have to be careful not to wake them, and she took a deep breath as she reached out again.

At the same time, Jill was telling Jack, "I am a professional woman. And I don't have time to be at home with diapers and baby socks."

"You don't have to, Jill," he told her. "I'll be the stay-at-home dad."

"Well, guess what, Mr Mom, we've got ten hungry piggies in the back, so why don't you pull on over and feed 'em," she said.

"I fed 'em this morning." He paused. "I *think*."

"See, you're already shirking," groaned Jill. "Just pull up ahead."

Puss whispered to Kitty as soon as he heard that. "You've got to hurry it up!"

"Shhh!" Kitty told him as she pulled out her dagger.

Puss stared at her, confused. "Why are you not using your claws?" he whispered.

"Would you please just shut up? I'm on it!"

"Just use your claws!" he hissed.

"Be quiet!"

"Your claws!"

Kitty gritted her teeth. "I don't have any claws, all right?" she confessed bitterly to him.

Suddenly, one of the piglets snorted awake. Puss and Kitty both froze as it started to squirm.

"Was that Hamhock?" they heard Jill asking Jack.

The cats knew they had to do something *fast*!

First, Puss let Kitty fall into the wagon, where she rushed to the piglet and scooped it up. "There, there. Sleepy, sleepy, big, fat piggie," she cooed as she rocked the fat, bristly baby back and forth.

Puss, meanwhile, jumped down, too, and swiftly opened the lock on Jack's box with his claws. Then very, *very* carefully he unfolded the steel from around Jack's hand.

In the driver's seat, Jack and Jill were still talking.

"Why don't we start with a fish, make sure you don't do anything to it, and build from there. Remember when we had to pretend we had that monkey that time, and it threw doo-doo all over the house? It's going to be the same thing with a baby, Jack."

"When did we have a monkey?"

"I put a lot of work into my body. This is what

we call hereditary. I look good. There go my jeans."

"Pumpkin, you look more beautiful than the day we met."

Down in the wagon, Puss drew a deep breath. *Ah! The beans! At last!* He licked his paws in anticipation. But before Puss could slip the magic beans from Jack's clenched fingers, Kitty handed him the pig.

"You babysit," she whispered as she pulled off her gloves. She winked. "Soft paws," she reminded him, waving the clawless tips, and Puss held his breath as he watched her move in.

A moment later, she leaned back.

"Well?" Puss asked.

Kitty grinned and unfurled her paw to reveal three magical, glowing beans.

"Hello, beans of legend!" Puss gasped as she poured them into his paw. He gulped, taking a moment to let it all sink in. Then he finally nodded to Kitty. "Let's go," he said.

But no sooner did Puss step back than his

boot came down on a sleeping piglet's tail. The piglet woke up at once with an ear-piercing "SQUEEEEAAL!" This instantly woke up the others and soon the wagon was filled with them. Then came a deep "HOWL!" from Puss when an angry piglet sank his teeth into his leg.

Kitty looked up just in time to see the door they'd come through slam shut with a BANG! They heard a ratcheting sound next, then a series of clanks and clangs. And the next thing they knew, the front of the wagon fell open and Jack and Jill's driver's seats spun around!

CHAPTER

SEVEN

"Well, well, well." Jack nodded at Puss, sneering. "Look what we have here, Jill. Housekeeping. Ha!"

Jack laughed at his own joke while Jill looked down at the piglet whose jaws were still clamped around Puss's boot. Her face twisted into a furious snarl. "You messed with my baby," she growled.

"And you took my beans." Jack's eyes narrowed as he noticed the glow coming from Puss's paw.

Jack stood up from his seat and moved toward the cats, pulling a knife from his belt as he did.

In turn, Puss drew his sword and held it to the piglet that was *still* biting him.

Jack stopped, and Kitty saw her chance to turn the tables on the thieves. "Sausage bomb!" she cried, grabbing the piglet from Puss's boot. She hurled it at Jack, who dropped his knife so that he could catch it in his arms. At the same moment, Kitty jumped on Jack, who fell straight back into his seat.

Puss threw his sword at the captain's chair lever, which caused the seats to jerk skyward, back up through the roof.

"Oh, you're going to pay for this! Soul-sucking cats!" Jill cursed.

When Puss jammed the gears so the seats were stuck, Kitty jumped off Jack to open the trap door of the roof and pull Puss up with a rope. They used the same rope to tie the thieves to their chairs as the wagon sped down the pass.

"Signal the egg!" Puss yelled finally.

Kitty nodded and pulled out a small mirror and held it up to the sun. From his lookout high in the canyon, Humpty could see the flash of the sunlight reflected. Yes! *His* turn had come!

Soon Humpty was pulling up to Jack and Jill's wagon in a stagecoach of his own. Puss and Kitty crouched, ready to spring as soon as the stage got close enough.

"OK," Kitty said.

"Ready . . ." Humpty yelled.

"Set . . ." Kitty called.

"Go!" squawked Jill's shrill voice as she managed to rear back in her seat just far enough to give Puss a nasty head butt.

Kitty made it safely to the stagecoach, but Puss went sailing back across the wagon roof. Dazed, he sat up slowly, only to see that he'd dropped the beans! He lunged out frantically to grab them as they bounced, just out of reach. But before he could grab them, the world went dark. The wagon had plunged into a tunnel. Fortunately, the beans still glowed and Puss could see them shining like fat green stars. *Un*fortunately, Jill was free by that time. She had gnawed straight through her rope.

The next instant, the wagon burst out of the

tunnel back into the daylight, and for a second Puss had to cover his eyes. When he took his paw away, he froze. Jill was standing over him with a stick, like a snake poised to strike. Puss unfroze and rolled to the side, just in time to get out of the way of Jill's deadly swing. The stick whished by him and hit Jack in his meaty face instead.

Madly, Puss scrambled for the beans, which were still bouncing across the wagon roof. He managed to get two, but just before he could reach the third bean, it bounded up and over the side. Desperately, Puss lunged for it . . . and caught it just in time! But then Jill caught *him*, and the next thing he knew, she was dangling him up by the throat. Tears filled Puss's eyes. (Mostly from her breath, but he was a little nervous, too).

By then Jack had also freed himself and was finally taking back the reins. Seeing a rock wall ahead, he steered his team of wild hogs toward it.

"Hey, Jill!" he yelled.

She looked over and saw where Jack was heading and held Puss out over the wagon's side. "You've got ten seconds, cat. Give me them beans!" she barked. "Nine, eight, five—"

"What happened to six and seven?" Puss asked.

She sneered and continued. "Four, three, two—"

And then, as if from out of nowhere, Humpty's stagecoach appeared alongside.

"Hang on!" Humpty cried as he drove the stage into Jack and Jill's wagon, knocking it away from the canyon wall.

"*One!*" shouted Jill, ready to drop Puss.

"*Heeyah!*" Humpty cried. He gave one more hard slap to the reins and the horse pulling the stage surged forward, bumping the wagon and causing Jill to lose her grip. The next thing Puss knew, he could feel himself falling . . . and falling . . . onto the stagecoach.

He was safe – for now.

The next minute, the canyon wall split the trail in two, and the two wagons continued on opposite sides. It took Puss a moment to catch his breath and realize that he was, in fact, alive. He pulled up his boots and checked his sword, and smiled down at the beans glowing safe in his paw. Then he peered over the roof to Humpy in the driver's seat below.

"See, I told you I wouldn't let you down," Humpty said, flashing Puss the same grin he remembered from when they were young.

Puss smiled back and hopped down to the seat between Humpty and Kitty and opened his hand. "We got them!" he said, giddily. "We got—"

BAM!

The three looked over to see a hole blasted clear through the wall of rock.

"You just picked a fight with the wrong outlaw!" Jill cackled as she fired another cannonball. In fact, by then she'd unfolded the side of their wagon to reveal a whole row of giant guns.

"Hey! That was close!" Humpty hollered and he cracked the reins urgently. *"Heeyah!"*

Moments later, the canyon trail converged

once more and the wagons were side by side again. Back and forth, they traded slams in a struggle to knock the other one off the road. Eventually, the trail curved, and suddenly they were riding along a cliff. Puss and Humpty peered over the side. They had the misfortune to be closest to the edge.

"Now!" Jill called to Jack, who swerved in a mighty effort to push the stagecoach off the trail. And it nearly worked. The stage swung out and Puss looked down. There was nothing beneath them but a thousand feet of air!

"That's it, I'm driving!" Puss shouted to Humpty.

But Humpty drove on, determined and grim. He nodded ahead to another gap where the struts of an old bridge could be seen. "We just have to make it to that bridge!" he yelled, snapping the reins again. "Hang on!"

But as they got closer, Puss realized something most distressing that made his fur stand straight up. The deck of the bridge had fallen away. There was nothing ahead but a steep drop!

"Humpty, there is no bridge!" Puss cried, pointing. But the egg charged on at full speed.

"Trust me," he said, his eyes gleaming. But it was all Puss could do not to scream.

Jack and Jill had just realized the bridge was out too, and Puss watched as they slid to a stop just short of the edge. But Humpty hadn't slowed down at all. Had the egg lost his mind?

"Humpty!" Kitty and Puss called desperately. But by then, they knew it was too late.

The next moment, they were soaring off the end of the bridge, hurtling over the cliff.

"We're going to die!" wailed Puss. He never dreamed he'd go like this . . .

CHAPTER
EIGHT

Slowly, Puss opened his eyes. They should have hit the ground by then . . .

Then he looked around. They were *flying*! Puss couldn't believe it!

Then he suddenly remembered all those plans Humpty had worked on, including ones for a wagon with wings. He looked out at the wings that now stretched from each side of the stage. The egg had actually built one! "Humpty, you did it!" Puss exclaimed.

The egg beamed. *"We* did it," Humpty said.

Gradually, he guided the winged stage down toward the ground, where they landed with a gentle bump on soft desert sand.

"Giant's castle, here we come," declared Humpty as they began to roll along the solid earth again.

After a few miles, the egg handed the reins to Puss and moved to the back of the stage. He had some serious navigating to do if they were going to find their way.

"East! Are we going east?" he called to Puss.

Puss studied the sun. "*Sí*, Humpty."

"Four miles, divide by cloud weight, account for circumference . . . OK, we should be close! Keep your eyes out for any strange cloud activity!" Humpty called.

"I must hand it to the egg," Puss told Kitty, who was still seated by his side, "this was a team effort. Humpty still has his claws—" Oops! Puss bit his lip. "I mean *flaws* – was what I meant."

He winced as Kitty flashed him a cool look. He hadn't meant to bring up that *claw* thing, though it was still on his mind.

"Not *claws*. He is not a cat. *Heh*. Uh, not to

say there is anything wrong—"

"I don't want to talk about it," Kitty cut in. Frowning, she looked away.

Puss nodded. "Got it."

"Make a left here!" Humpty called from the back.

Puss leaned into Kitty as he steered the wagon, and smiled at her awkwardly as they straightened up.

She smiled back and eyed him slyly. "I am called Kitty Softpaws because I'll steal you blind, and you'll never even know I was there."

Then she held up Puss's coin purse. He frowned and snatched it back from her.

"Kitty, you are not as good as they say. You are better," Puss declared. "I will respect your privacy," he went on, nodding. Then he began to whistle . . . sorely off-key.

Kitty sighed. "OK, fine, I'll tell you."

Puss turned, surprised, but quite eager to hear.

"I was just a stray," Kitty began wistfully.

"But I had beautiful claws. One day a really nice couple took me in, gave me milk every morning. Loved me." She paused. "Maybe I scratched their curtains or chased too many mice . . . I don't know why they did it." She sniffed. "But they took my claws."

For a moment, Puss was speechless. He had no words for the horror she had been through.

"Cat people are crazy," he said finally.

Kitty nodded, and for a while the two fell silent. There was no sound except for the rumble of the coach travelling on the dusty ground.

Then all of a sudden, Humpty popped out from the behind the curtain that separated the front seat from the back of the stage. "Stop! Stop the coach!" he shouted. "I think this is it!"

Puss pulled the reins hard, then turned to see the stage door swing open before they'd even stopped. Out hopped the egg, armed with a shovel and map. He quickly waddled off.

Puss and Kitty turned to each other, then they hopped down and followed him. By the time they caught up, Humpty had stopped running and was practically glowing as he gazed into Puss's face.

"Can you believe this, Puss?" he asked, ecstatic. "After all these years? Here." He held out the magic beans to Puss. "I want you to plant them."

"No, no, Humpty." Puss shook his head. "This was your dream," he told the egg.

"It was *our* dream, Puss," Humpty reminded him. He poured the beans into Puss's paw. "I insist."

Puss looked down and then back up at Humpty, and then it hit him: They were friends again. Their whole troubled past, it was all water under the bridge.

Just then Kitty pointed up to the sky. "That is a strange cloud," she observed.

Puss and Humpty followed her clawless paw. Yes, it certainly was. The cloud wasn't just big, it was swirling, almost like a whirlpool in the sky. As they watched, it spun and grew until it had completely covered the sun.

"Whoa, OK! This is it," Humpty cried happily.

He was practically jumping out of his shell. "It's happening. Hurry!" he urged the cats.

Keeping a watchful eye on the turbulent sky, he led Puss and Kitty to a clearing not too far away. "Good, good," he said. "Come on, come on, come on." Then he gestured for Puss to hold the beans up as high as he could.

Puss did . . . and in an instant, the air seemed to take on an electric charge.

"OK, good! Good," Humpty panted as the cloud above began to rumble and churn. "Twenty-three, divided by cloud depth." He tossed his pencil to the ground. "Hole! Right here."

Kitty moved to the spot where the pencil had landed, point first and quickly began to dig a hole.

"Now place the beans . . ." he instructed Puss, breathlessly. "Carefully, please!" he warned. "Not on top of one another. The magic is very delicate."

Puss flashed him a look as he bent over the ground. How hard was it, really, to put beans in a hole?

"OK, good." Humpty sighed. "Very good. Now

just stand back," he said at last.

Puss and Kitty each took a step back while Humpty carefully covered the beans with dirt and gave them a gentle pat. Then the egg stepped back as well, and their eyes all drifted up. By then, the cloud had filled the sky and grown so dark that it was black. Forks of lightning flashed from its turbulent heart as the canyon walls began to shake. From the rumbling earth, a stream of energy shot straight up into space. A jagged crack appeared in the ground exactly where Puss had planted the beans. And with a mighty *THHHPPPPTTT!* the earth opened up . . .

And a tiny green sprout popped out of it.

Huh? Puss leaned in closer. Really? Was that *it*?

Humpty stepped up with his hands on his wide, round hips. "What's happening here?" he asked, concerned.

Puss shrugged. "Maybe the magic rubbed off in your pocket?" he said.

Humpty shook his head. "Impossible." He frowned and began to turn red.

"OK, OK, let's not panic," said Kitty. She rubbed her chin and tried to think. "You know, I read somewhere that plants have feelings," she said. "So, come on." She pointed to the scrawny stem. "Say something nice to it."

Puss scoffed and rolled his eyes, but Humpty was desperate enough to give it a try.

"OK, let me think for a second . . . Hi, little plant—"

KA-BOOM!

Like a volcano, the ground erupted at once, and an enormous beanstalk shot out. It grew so fast, it caught the egg and the cats in its leaves, and carried them up at rocket-ship speed.

Puss looked down. How fast were they going? A thousand feet a second, at least! The earth below was getting smaller. The desert canyons already looked like tiny cracks. And the stalk was getting wider, twisting and writhing as if it were alive. It snapped and creaked as it coiled and bent and stretched, and its leaves rustled like thunder as the wind rushed by.

Several times Puss found himself tumbling from one leaf to another as the vine grew . . . and grew . . . and grew. The plant tossed him around like a cat toy, no matter how hard he tried to hold on. He became tangled in a tendril at one point with Kitty – which actually wasn't so bad. But the next thing Puss knew, a new stem sprang out, carrying the two cats miles apart. At least when they reached the clouds, the stalk began to slow. But the clouds they had passed through had left Puss miserably soaked.

Finally, they plunged into the upper atmosphere. The Earth looked like a hazy marble far below. There was a shock of snow, then a blast of sunlight and finally, a jarring jolt as they came to a stop.

"Uh, guys?" Humpty peered out of the leaf he had clung to for most of the ride.

Slowly, the cats peeked over their leaves too. "*Aah!*" they all gasped. There was nothing but clouds all around them. It was a landscape made entirely of white.

Humpty scrambled up, then slid down off his leaf, disappearing – *PLOOF!* – in a fluffy mound of pure white mist.

"Humpty!" cried Kitty and Puss, anxiously.

"I do not see him. Do you see him?" Puss asked.

Kitty looked all around. "I don't see him anywhere," she said.

Then Puss turned to her. "You sound weird," he said. And come to think of it, so did he. Their voices were thin and much higher than normal, as if they'd been breathing in pure helium.

"It's the thin air," Humpty's own tinny voice informed them as he burst back up into view. "Come on in! It feels great!" He laughed and giddily dove back in.

Puss and Kitty shrugged and jumped in too. Wow! It was a feeling Puss had never felt before. "The cloud, it tickles my nose," he said and giggled.

"That's because they effervesce!" explained Humpty. "Who knew?"

Puss ducked as Kitty tossed a cloud ball at him. Then he laughed and tossed one back at her. Soon they were playing tag like a pair of kittens. Puss hadn't had this much fun in . . . ever, perhaps.

"Hey, Puss!" Humpty popped up with a full cloud moustache and beard that made him look like a Santa egg. "What do you think? Do I shave?"

Puss grinned and laughed. "Let me show you something," Humpty went on, shaking the cloud from his face. He bent down and parted the cloud floor with his hands so they could see the Earth below. "Somewhere down there, there are two little kids, I don't know, maybe orphans." He sighed. "And they're laying on a hill staring at the clouds, dreaming about the future. That was me and you, Puss. Me and you."

Suddenly Kitty called out, "Boys! You might want to take a look at this."

CHAPTER
NINE

"Look!" Kitty pointed to a place where the cloud mist was drifting away.

Puss stared as a massive structure came into view. It was a huge castle! And it was hovering in the sky, thanks to giant propellers on its base.

"The Giant's castle!" Humpty gasped.

Puss put his paw around the egg. "It's just how you described it when we were kids," he said.

"Exactly . . ." Humpty gazed at it longingly, almost hypnotized. Then at last, he shook the trance away. He clapped his hands and turned to his partners. "OK, time to suit up," he said. With that, he tossed his hat aside and began ripping off his trousers.

"Humpty!" Puss cried out, alarmed. This was more of his friend than he cared to see!

"Will you relax?" Humpty rolled his eyes and showed Puss that beneath his clothes he was wearing a tight gold body suit. He grabbed the top and tried to wriggle the skin-tight latex over his shell. Puss and Kitty watched uncomfortably as the egg fought the suit . . . and won at last.

Victorious, Humpty zipped the suit all the way up, to his eyeballs almost. Puss had to admit, Humpty looked a lot like a golden egg . . . from the front at least.

"Brilliant or what?" Humpty asked. "Wait! Where's my journal?" He spun around to reveal a book-shaped lump under his suit where his legs met his shell.

"Uh, Puss, can you give me a hand here?" he asked.

Puss sighed and did his best.

Soon the trio was winding their way through the clouds toward the castle.

"Puss, remember when everyone was laughing at Bean Club?" Humpty asked.

"And who is laughing now? Ha! We are!" Puss said.

"So am I in Bean Club now?" asked Kitty.

"Of course you are!" Puss told her. "You helped to steal the beans. Right, Humpty?"

But Humpty frowned. "Actually, technically, it's just me and Puss."

He stepped on a rising cloud, while Kitty waited for the next one to come. "Well, I never wanted to be in your Bean Gang anyway," she said indignantly, crossing her paws.

"Come on, Humpty," Puss pleaded. What was the big deal?

"What? It's not special if everybody's in it!" Humpty declared. Then he made the mistake of looking at Puss. He sighed at the sight of Puss's big, sad, amber eyes. "Fine. We'll make some sort of, I don't know, amendment to the rules."

"Wow." Kitty gasped just then as they finally reached the castle. Their clouds delivered them gently to a broad stone balcony. An enormous stained glass window rose before them with an elaborate golden goose design. It was all that separated them now from whatever wonders waited inside.

They discovered a gap in the window that was large enough for them to easily slip through. But once inside they had to stop for a moment just to take in the awesome view. The floor was hundreds of feet below them, and the ceiling was almost too high to see. The most amazing thing, though, was the actual *rainforest* that took up the entire centre of the great room. It was easily as big as San Ricardo, complete with towering trees and waterfalls that ran like columns from ceiling to floor.

Humpty gazed out and grinned. "That is our target," he said.

"Hey, you don't sound like an elf anymore," Kitty remarked.

Humpty nodded. "It's the jungle air." Then he took a deep breath. "Let's get to work."

It was a long, long way to the ground. Too far for them to jump, for sure. Fortunately there was a tapestry near the window that stretched all the way to the floor. It depicted a vicious battle scene among all sorts of horrible Giants. Humpty jumped on Puss's back, piggyback style, while Puss climbed down the tapestry using his claws. Kitty, meanwhile, whipped out two razor-sharp daggers and used them instead of claws.

Puss tried not to focus on the bloodthirsty giants as he made his way down the tapestry, but they were impossible to ignore. "OK, where is the Giant?" he finally asked Humpty, his voice full of dread.

"The Giant's been dead for years," replied Humpty.

Puss turned around to stare at him. "What do you mean the Giant is dead?"

"You didn't do the reading, did you?" said

Humpty. "Oh boy. *Jack and the Beanstalk,* Chapter Fourteen. 'Giant Takes a Big Dirt Nap'?"

"How did he die?" Puss asked as they reached the floor.

Humpty jumped off, and Puss stretched, glad to have the egg off his back. But before Humpty could answer him, a horrible wail and an ominous rumble made Puss crouch and look around.

"Does that answer your question?" said Humpty. "*She* did it."

"Who?" Puss asked.

"The Great Terror who watches over the Golden Goose," Humpty said. He nodded toward the jungle. "Follow me and keep quiet," he told the cats. Then he waddled ahead, and Puss and Kitty cringed at a new and equally disturbing, stretchy sound.

Ugh! What was it? Puss watched Humpty take another step, and then he instantly knew.

"Shhh! Humpty!" he whispered.

"It's not me, it's this body stocking," Humpty replied. The egg tugged at his stretchy gold middle, but there wasn't much he could do.

He squeaked and waddled up to an old empty wine bottle. "There it is." He sighed, peering around.

The egg gazed longingly at the lush rainforest before them. It seemed to grow out of its own island and was surrounded by a deep moat. An oasis of life in the otherwise desolate castle, its bright foliage and refreshing waterfalls beckoned them to explore. At the same time, though, another haunting wail from deep within made the dangers awaiting them there all too real.

"It's the Garden of the Golden Goose," Humpty said, in awe. He pointed gravely to the moat. "We've got to get across."

The three scanned the dusty stone floor around them until an unopened champagne bottle caught their eye. Together, they rolled it carefully toward the edge of the moat. "Easy . . . whoa!" Humpty warned suddenly. But he was too late. They accidentally bumped an empty wine glass and knocked it over the edge. The egg and the cats watched in agony as it disappeared . . . and soon shattered far below.

In response, from deep inside the mist-shrouded forest, another howl drifted out. Instantly all three explorers went pale. What kind of beast could make that sound? None of them wanted to face it. But how could they turn back now?

"OK. Let's go!" Humpty said finally, taking a deep breath to steady his nerves. He shoved the bottle so it lined up facing the forest, while Puss and Kitty climbed up onto the neck. They shimmied along till they reached the cork, then Puss drew his sword and plunged it in. Then he and Kitty both tied a rope around their waists and tossed the other end to Humpty, who tied it securely to a rock. Together, Puss and Kitty grabbed the cork with their arms, and at the same time pushed against the top of the bottle, hard, with their legs. Little by little, they could feel the cork loosening up . . . until the whole bottle began to shake. They pushed . . . and pushed with all their might until – *POP!* – the cork shot out.

The next thing they knew, Puss and Kitty were sailing across the moat on the cork . . . up, up, and over the waterfalls.

"Yes!" Humpty cried, pumping his fist as he watched them land safely in the thick jungle brush.

No sooner had Puss and Kitty climbed to their feet, however, when there was another bloodcurdling *"R-r-r-ooooar!"*

Gallantly, Puss threw Kitty behind him. "Do not worry. I will protect you!" he said.

"What are you going to do?" teased Kitty. "Hit it on the head with a guitar?"

Puss hung his head and mumbled, "Please stop bringing up the guitar."

They took the cork they had flown across the moat on and wedged it tightly between two trees. Then they tied their ropes around some thick branches and signalled to Humpty that it was safe for him to proceed.

All Humpty had to do then was zipline across. But that was a lot easier said than done. The

Far from Puss In Boots's hometown of San Ricardo, the outlaw entered the saloon.

A man told Puss that Jack and Jill had found the legendary magic beans that would lead to finding the Golden Goose. If Puss could get the beans, he could pay back San Ricardo with golden eggs!

Jack and Jill were keeping the magic beans safe in a locked box at a hotel across town.

Puss snuck into their room at the same time as a masked stranger who was also after the magic beans. They fled when Jack fired a shot . . .

Puss followed the masked
stranger into an underground
cat cantina.

They duelled in a dance fight, matching each other move for move, until Puss hit the masked stranger in the face with a guitar.

Puss was surprised to find out that the stranger was a female, Kitty Softpaws.

Kitty led Puss to a friend who had betrayed him long ago – Humpty Alexander Dumpty.

Humpty and Kitty were working together. They had a plan to get the magic beans, but they needed Puss's help.

But could he trust Humpty? There was only one way to find out. Soon Puss, Humpty and Kitty were planting the magic beans and climbing the beanstalk as it raced into the sky.

Puss In Boots wanted nothing more than to put his days as an outlaw behind him and return to the village of San Ricardo as a hero . . . and all he needed was a golden egg.

minute Humpty pushed off the ledge of the great hall, deep, dark, paralyzing fear of falling came rushing over him.

"Catch me!" he cried as he slid down the rope, but it slackened before he cleared the gap. Gradually, he slowed as he neared the jungle side . . . until he was stuck, mere feet from the edge.

"Humpty!" called both Puss and Kitty. He was so close to safety and to them.

They reached out, but the egg had his eyes shut tight. He was frozen, too scared to move. In his mind, he was remembering himself as a small egg, falling helplessly through space. It was a vision so real and terrifying, and he eventually started to scream.

"Ahhhh!"

"Humpty!" Finally, Puss's voice broke though his nightmare and Humpty opened his eyes. He looked down to see the jungle ground beneath him and Puss and Kitty smoothly reeling him in.

He swallowed hard, embarrassed. "I-I d-don't

understand what's going on," he stammered. "It's probably the suit."

"Quietly," Puss reminded him, gently helping him to the safety – he hoped – of a nearby hollow log.

"The suit's tight," Humpty panted. "I'm sweating."

Then all of a sudden, the ground began to rumble and the trees around them began to shake. The ghostly wail pierced their ears again. Whatever was making that sound was very big . . . and very close, apparently!

"Humpty, be quiet!" warned Kitty.

The egg nodded, then he peeked out of the log. "I've been here before," he muttered, bewildered. Everything looked strangely familiar to him.

"Hey, you've got to get it together," Puss told him. This was definitely no time for the egg to start losing his head.

"OK." Humpty nodded and took a deep breath, trying to focus on the job at hand. He guessed the whole experience was so intense, it was causing his mind to play tricks on him.

CHAPTER
TEN

Puss, Humpty and Kitty made their way, like ants, through the giant jungle, through ferns as thick and high as trees. Vines grew in dense tangles, and Puss's and Kitty's swords stayed busy hacking them out of the way. How much farther till they found the Golden Goose? Puss wondered. And how long before the Great Terror found them?

Then suddenly the jungle gave way to a far different landscape – a field dotted with enormous eggs made entirely of pure gold.

"Whoa!" Puss's eyes practically popped out at the sight of the treasure before them.

"There's enough gold here to pay back San Ricardo and his Mama," Humpty crowed.

Gleefully, he slid down a steep slope from the jungle into the field and sidled up to an egg. He leaned over and kissed it, cooing, "I love you so much!" Then he stood up and wrapped his arm around the golden orb, which was every bit as big as him.

"Grab as many as you can," he called to Puss and Kitty. Then he groaned as he struggled to move just one.

Puss tried to lift one as well. "I thought they were going to be, like, chicken-sized," he moaned.

"Can you imagine laying one of these?" said Kitty. She tried to help Puss, but the egg barely budged.

"Puss! Owww!" they heard Humpty holler.

Puss and Kitty dashed over to find Humpty on his back, pinned under a shiny egg. The cats put their paws on the egg and pushed . . . and pushed as hard as they could until it rolled off Humpty at last.

"How are we supposed to get these out of here?" Puss asked.

"I don't know," Humpty said with a heavy, but still happy sigh.

HONK-HONK!

Their heads spun at once at a sound in the distance.

"Oh my . . ." Humpty gasped, jumping up.

"The Golden Goose." Puss stared in awe at the magnificent bird. It was every bit as bright as the eggs she was laying as she ambled through the field.

"Just look at her. Isn't she beautiful?" said Humpty as the goose made her way toward them. When she finally reached Humpty, she gave him a friendly peck. "Oh. Oh, my sweet darling!" he exclaimed, wrapping his arms around her neck.

K-R-R-A-A-A-CK!

"Humpty, quiet!" Puss hissed. The jungle was rumbling again. The Great Terror was approaching, snapping trees like matchsticks as she did.

"Let's just take her," Humpty said, grinning. His arms were still wrapped around the goose's neck.

"Wait a minute." Puss raised a cautious paw. "This is the goose of legend. We don't know what happens if we take her," he said.

"Well, I know what happens if we don't take her – we get nothing!" Humpty quickly replied.

Another awful wail echoed through the jungle just then, making the team of three cringe.

"Just take the goose, Puss. Do it!" Humpty snapped.

Kitty nodded. "OK, I'm with Humpty. Let's just please get out of here," she urged.

"Do it for San Ricardo! For Imelda!" Humpty begged.

Another *"R-R-ROAAARR!"* shook the forest.

Puss winced and took a deep, dread-filled breath. Taking the Golden Goose was the only way, he nervously agreed.

Moments later, the three were racing back through the jungle to their zipline, though they weren't alone this time. The Golden Goose was strapped to Puss's back and honking away happily. The only problem was that her squawking was guiding the Great Terror straight toward them!

Behind them, trees collapsed as the Terror closed in. Finally, the egg and the cats reached the edge of the forest and the awaiting zipline, and one by one they jumped on.

"Almost there!" hollered Humpty as they worked their way, hand over hand, back across.

And then suddenly, to their horror, the champagne bottle started to slide toward the moat! They could feel the line getting more and more slack, and soon saw the bottle teeter just at the edge. Their hearts leaped to their throats as it began to fall over.

"Hang on!" Humpty called as their rope followed it into the abyss.

CRASH!

The bottom of the bottle slammed into the

side of the moat and shattered, but luckily for the team, the neck stayed intact. Humpty, Kitty, and Puss slid down the rope and clung to the slick glass surface with every muscle they had. Startled, the Golden Goose, who was still strapped to Puss's back, honked and laid an egg right there, in midair.

"Shut that bird up!" snapped Humpty, shooting the goose a sharp, annoyed glare.

THUMP-THUMP!

Their ears pricked at the sound of heavy footsteps. The beast was right above them, they could tell. But it also seemed to be moving away. They looked around at each other hopefully and shared a timid grin.

"I think we're OK," Humpty said as, together, they let out a sigh of relief.

But no sooner had their breaths left their bodies than a deafening "*ROAR!*" filled the air once again. The next thing they knew, their zipline jerked straight up at a fur-raising, shell-shocking pace. The Great Terror had them caught like fish on a hook!

There was nothing to do but scream *"HELP!"*

Then they saw it: a huge, craggy root jutting out from the side of the moat, just below the jungle's edge. Desperate, they grabbed for it, leaving the broken bottle to continue its ascent. Then they listened to the monster howl as it discovered its prey was gone. Bitterly, the Great Terror hurled the bottle back over the edge, into the moat. Shards of broken glass flew around the trio like daggers, and the earth shook as the monster threw a fit. After a moment, the explorers looked at one another, knowing that they had little choice but to slide down into the moat.

The bottom of the moat was even damper and denser than the jungle they'd left above. Puss, Kitty and Humpty looked around. The goose on Puss's back let out a curious "honk." *Where do we go now?* they wondered. The place was a treacherous web of vines and roots hiding infinite dangers as bad as those they'd just left . . . or maybe worse. But no, on second thought, nothing could be as deadly as the Great Terror who, it seemed, was far from giving up.

"It's coming!" cried Humpty, the dirt raining down on them as the monster careened down the moat's walls in pursuit.

Then suddenly – *BOOM! SPLASH!* – a pair of monstrous feet the size of school buses landed in a muddy river not too far away. The team froze, their jaws wide open.

Frantically, they scrambled away from the monster, along the river, clinging to vines so they wouldn't fall in. But a falling branch knocked Kitty off balance. She screamed and grabbed at the vine with her paws. Puss turned and saw her and dropped the goose.

"Kitty!" he called, rushing back.

"I'm fine, just go!" she told him.

Then she let go.

"What are you doing?!" Puss cried.

He watched as she fell into the river and was swiftly swept away. Downstream, Kitty grabbed for another vine with her soft paws and struggled to hold on. But the monster was bearing down on her and before she knew it, she looked up, and there was the beast.

Then suddenly Puss's head popped up out of the water beside her, and he grabbed her and pulled her down.

Humpty, meanwhile, was floating along in his jumpsuit, which he'd inflated by pulling a cord. He paddled frantically after the Golden Goose. "Come here, you!" he called.

Puss and Kitty resurfaced downriver only to discover a giant whirlpool at the end.

"Hang on!" Puss hollered as the water spun around like a washing machine, quickly sucking them in.

Humpty lunged for the goose as he followed them. "I got you!" he yelled. Then, just before he disappeared down the whirlpool's vortex, the Great Terror almost landed on top of him.

Humpty looked up into the monster's bright eye with a devilish grin. "She's mine now!" he taunted as the enraged monster roared and hissed.

CHAPTER
ELEVEN

"AHHH!" cried Humpty as the whirlpool spun him like a top. He held the Golden Goose tight in his spindly arms. Moments later, he and Puss and Kitty were gone – like goldfish flushed down a deep toilet bowl.

The next thing they knew, the cats and the egg spilled out of the castle. In fact, the whirlpool had been some sort of giant drain. They landed on the beanstalk, but with so much force that it was impossible to stop themselves.

Humpty quickly tumbled down, and for a second, found himself fluttering *over* the goose before he was able to clamber onto its back.

But then the goose kept falling!

"No! No! Fly little gosling! Fly!" Humpty yelled. The goose just stared at him oddly, however, and honked without moving its wings at all.

"No! No!" Humpty wailed as they dropped. "It's not supposed to be this way! *Ahhh!!*" Humpty had everything he wanted – and now he was about to lose it all. Then he felt a tug on his ankle. "Puss?" he gasped, looking down.

"No."

It was Kitty, wide-eyed and scared for her own life. There seemed to be no way to stop their free fall . . .

Then suddenly they heard a friendly whistle. It was Puss! He'd fashioned a hang-glider out of a leaf that he'd cut off of a stalk with his sword, and now he was sailing toward his friends, ready to rescue them. Unfortunately his aim was slightly off.

BAM! Puss accidentally flew into Humpty and knocked him out of Kitty's grip. Kitty grabbed on to Puss's leaf, but it was no longer working like a wing.

"Uh, I am sorry," Puss said as the ground zoomed up before them at a most alarming rate. But Kitty just frowned and very calmly grabbed the other end of the leaf. Together, they stabilized and swooped back up toward Humpty, and they each grabbed a thin leg in their paw. Then they gently sailed back down, circling around the giant beanstalk.

"We did it! We did it!" cried Humpty.

Kitty smiled and winked at Puss. Then she banked the glider so he slid into her. "Thanks for saving me, Ginger. I owe you one," she said.

Puss smiled, full of pride . . . and another feeling, too. It was a strange but thrilling one. Something fresh and new.

Humpty, meanwhile, stared at the beanstalk as they flew by . . .

"Um," he said. "We should maybe cut that down."

Jack and Jill, meanwhile, bumped along through the desert in their wobbly wagon, determined to chase down their beans.

Jill carried her favourite piglet on her lap. "Kiss, kiss, little Hamhock," she cooed. "Give Mama a little kiss on the lips." She puckered up and gave the little pig's snout a smooch. Then she held it up to Jack. "Somebody's getting a little neck wash," she said. The piglet squealed and grunted happily, then began to root around the dirty folds of Jack's thick, sweaty neck.

"Ha!" Jack laughed fondly. "He's been eating possum again."

He chuckled as they drove on, before noticing something sparkling in the sand just ahead. Jill followed his gaze, and even Hamhock's beady red eyes zeroed in. Jack and Jill turned to each other. He raised an eyebrow; she curled her lip. Was it a clue? Jack snapped the reins and steered the wagon towards it.

When they reached the shiny object, Jill took the reins and Jack climbed down. He frowned as he picked up Humpty's telescope.

"Well, what is it?" Jill asked.

Jack shrugged and turned the long, brass tube over in his hand. He'd never seen anything like it before. He held it up and peered through one end.

Then he squinted. What was *that*? An enormous plant rushing toward him?

WHOMP!

He lowered the telescope just as the giant beanstalk crashed next to him. A dust cloud enveloped them immediately, then slowly settled. Jack coughed before climbing back into his seat. "I do believe that's our cue," he told Jill, snapping angrily at the reins. *"Haw!"*

Of course, as far as Puss and his teammates were concerned, their troubles were over. Mission accomplished! What could go wrong?

As evening fell, they made a campfire and celebrated.

"Woo-hoo!" Humpty cheered as the Golden Goose laid another priceless egg. He hoisted one up ecstatically . . . then toppled over under its weight.

Puss and Kitty hardly noticed though. They were far too busy replaying their "dance fight" from the day that they met. This time, however, their dancing had a much more . . . *romantic* twist to it. Their eyes were locked on each other's, and their feet seemed to be exchanging messages of love. In fact, their dancing brought them so close that that by the end, they'd traded boots.

"Kitty," Puss said, admiringly, "I knew that when I first met you, we would make a good team."

"You mean when I picked your pocket?" She batted her eyelashes and held up his coin pouch.

Puss nodded, grinning, and tipped his hat to her, revealing a pile of safely stowed coins underneath.

As Humpty broke into a dance himself – a conga line with the goose – Puss twirled Kitty to the other side of the campfire and stared silently at her.

Almost nose to nose, Puss pulled Kitty in closer and closer . . . until Humpty twirled over and grabbed Kitty. As he danced away from Puss with Kitty in his arms, Humpty whispered furiously in her ear, "Let's stick with the plan!"

Moments later, Puss pulled Kitty back into his arms.

"Kitty, I was thinking, when we go our separate ways, we could go our separate ways *together*," he said.

"Puss . . ." she began, her eyes searching his.

He stroked her chin. "Kitty . . ."

Then suddenly she straightened up and pushed him away. "You have to go," she said matter-of-factly.

"You do not have to push me away anymore. You can trust me," he replied.

But before she could say any more, Humpty cut in again.

"Can you believe it, Puss? We went up the beanstalk outlaws and we came down legends!" he called, jumping between them for a high five.

Puss grinned and gave Humpty ten, while Kitty watched them with a sigh.

"I'm calling it a night, guys," she said solemnly.

Puss turned to her, disappointed. *Why so serious on such a night?* "Kitty, stay up with us," he begged her. But she shook her head. Puss supposed she was tired.

"Good night, Puss," she said softly.

He smiled and returned a warm "Good night."

As she left, Humpty settled down on a log by the campfire and motioned for Puss to sit by his side.

"Not bad for a couple of orphans, right?" said Humpty as Puss took a seat.

"I never thought we'd get here after all we went through. To pull this off together. It is good to have my brother back," Puss replied happily.

"Oh, Puss." Humpty grinned. "Just to hear you say those words . . . it's worth more than gold to me."

Side by side, they shared the moment, and then the egg stretched his scrawny arms and yawned. "We have a big day tomorrow. Pretty exciting stuff," he said. "We should get some rest." He pulled the drawstring on his gold suit snug, like a sleeping bag, up under his chin. Then he rolled off the log onto his side and closed his eyes.

"Good night, Humpty," Puss said fondly, as the Golden Goose hopped up on top of Humpty and closed her eyes too. Puss leaned back with his hands behind his head and gazed up at the twinkling night sky. A shooting star raced across the horizon.

"Canasta!" someone yelled.

That was the last thing Puss remembered before Jack knocked him out with a club.

The next thing Puss remembered was the blazing sun beating down on his face. It must have been high noon the next day.

Puss's eyes opened groggily, one by one. Crows were circling like vultures just above his head.

"Ahh! I'm still alive!" he cried, angrily swatting them away.

He rolled onto his stomach and winced. It

felt like his head was in a vise. Slowly, he rose to his feet looked and around. *What had happened there last night?*

The ground was tossed and rutted as if there'd been a struggle, that much was clear. But the campsite was empty. Kitty and Humpty were nowhere to be seen. All that was left was the smoldering fire, a grinning donkey, carriage tracks and two large sets of footprints trailing off across the sand. Puss studied them more closely and groaned as he realized they belonged to Jack and Jill.

"Kitty? Humpty?" he hollered, running after the tracks. He reached a ridge and could see they went on for miles. He clenched his paw in a fist and raised it. "I will find you," he swore bitterly.

CHAPTER
TWELVE

A donkey wasn't the fastest way to get across the desert, but it was better than going on foot.

"*Heeyah! Yah!*" Puss urged the donkey as they followed the wagon tracks across the sand. The donkey had one speed, however, and it was definitely not fast. Puss forged on, determined to save his friends.

At last, they passed a bush and Puss did a double take. *Was it? Yes.* It was Kitty's black mask! They were definitely on the right trail.

Puss gave the donkey another slap and urged him on again. But just then a huge dust cloud swept over them, leaving Puss and the donkey choking and blind. It took Puss a minute after the dust settled to clear all the sand from his eyes. When he finally did, he realized they'd reached a bridge to a village. He read the sign carved into the side: SAN RICARDO. His home. It had been so long since he left, but Puss remembered everything. It was like he'd never left . . . almost.

That's when a lone piece of paper, fluttering, nailed to the bridge caught Puss's eye, and he climbed down off the donkey to check it out. A lump caught in his throat as he read. It was a wanted poster – *his* wanted poster. He swallowed, and the lump sank to his stomach and slowly grew rock hard. But Puss squared his shoulders. He had to find his friends.

Hiding behind a rolling tumbleweed, Puss stealthily crept past the villagers and guards. When he finally reached a narrow alley, he slipped in and boldly slapped the tumbleweed and commanded it, "Be gone!"

As it rolled away obediently, Puss heard voices that made him peer down the street.

The voices belonged to Jack and Jill . . . and Humpty!

Puss gripped his sword, then he looked both ways to make sure the coast was clear. Moments later, he was standing in front of the group, brandishing his blade, ready to rescue Humpty.

Puss stared at what he saw before him, trying to comprehend it. He saw Jack and Jill and Humpty . . . with a bottle of champagne.

"What is going on?" he demanded.

Humpty smiled coolly at Puss. "Have you met my friends Jack and Jill?"

"Your friends?" Puss sputtered in disbelief as Jack and Jill burst into laughter.

"Maybe you guys should go," Humpty told Jack and Jill, and the pair hulked off, each carrying a gold egg.

"You set me up," gasped Puss as the truth sank in.

"Oh yes, I set you up!" Humpty spat back. "I set up everything. The magic beans, Jack and

Jill, Kitty. You know Kitty? Little bitty Kitty? It was all me."

Puss's face twisted in horror as he realized the scope of his friend's betrayal. "I trusted you!" he said angrily.

"Well, now you will know what it feels like to trust someone and have them stab you in the back!" Humpty retorted. "Guards!"

As if they were waiting – which they had been – armed guards poured into the square and surrounded Puss.

"I present to you the mastermind of the treasury break-in . . . Puss In Boots!" Humpty declared.

Puss aimed his sword at Humpty's chest. "I should scramble you with onions!" he angrily shouted.

Just then the Comandante stepped forward, his own sword drawn. "You are under arrest!" he informed Puss. Then he nodded to his guards.

Madly, Puss waved his sword, determined not to go down without a fight. But then a voice from the past called out to him . . . a very familiar voice he'd kept buried deep in his heart. "*Pequeño!* Wait." It was Imelda's. "Don't fight them, please!" she begged.

Imelda stepped up between Puss and the soldiers.

"Mama. Listen to me. I can explain," Puss began.

But she gave him a look so filled with disappointment that Puss couldn't help but lower his weapon and regretfully hang his head.

"Puss, no more running. No," said the old woman. "You must face what you have done."

Puss's furry chin trembled as he realized that she was right and that everything he'd done had been in vain. He sighed and let his sword fall to the cobblestones with a pitiful *plink*.

"I'm sorry, Mama," he muttered.

"Paws where we can see them," ordered a guard.

Puss obeyed and held his paws up.

"Turn around, slowly," the soldier went on.

Puss turned.

"Slower!" the guard shouted. Then he pointed to an open, cat-sized cage.

"Step into the carrier, quiet-like," commanded the Comandante.

Defeated and miserable, Puss dropped to all fours and did as the man said. By then, most of the town had gathered to see the historic capture of San Ricardo's most notorious thief. Inside the crate, Puss looked out through the bars at the people, ashamed – not just because of what he'd done, but because he'd trusted the egg. How could he have been so foolish as to put his life in those rotten hands?

At the same time, Humpty was delighting in the moment, revelling in the knowledge that his plan had worked. He stood in the center of the square and motioned for the villagers to gather all around.

"Attention, attention, everyone. If you could come in a little closer? For so very long, the only

121

wish I've had was to repay an old debt to San Ricardo and to my mum. And now I finally have my chance. Ladies and gentleman, I present to you the Golden Goose of legend!"

Then Puss was stunned as a black cat appeared with the goose on a leash. "Kitty," he murmured. Their eyes met for a moment before Kitty looked away uncomfortably. She led the goose up to Humpty who greeted it with a *"Boo!"*

"Honk!" The startled bird laid a golden egg right there in front of the astonished crowd.

"Perfect!" Humpty scooped it up and offered it to Imelda. "It's for you, Mum," he told her with a smile nearly as wide as his face.

The old woman took it . . . scowling suspiciously. The egg was up to *something*, she was positive, and knowing him, it was no good. But the rest of the crowd was already cheering. *"Viva el huevo! Long live the egg!"* There hadn't been that much gold in their sleepy, dusty town in years!

Puss listened to their joyful voices sadly as the guards loaded his carrier onto a wagon and drove away. Just the day before, he had thought a bright new future lay before him. Now he had lost everything . . .

"One hat. One belt. And two boots, once a symbol of honour." The Comandante shook his head. His eyes were full of disappointment as Puss stood before him, undressed. He handed Puss's possessions to another guard, then led Puss to a prison cell himself.

The Comandante opened the heavy barred door with a thick iron key, then he stood aside to let his guards toss the prisoner in. As soon as the cat was in the deep, dark cell, the Comandante slammed the door closed. "This is where you belong, outlaw," he told Puss through the bars. "And this is where you will stay forever."

With that, the guards marched away and Puss sank to the cold stone floor.

Hearing the sound of rattling chains, Puss turned, startled to discover another prisoner sharing his cell. He was an old-timer, clearly, with a white beard down to his waist. His clothes were scarcely more than rags, and his gnarled feet were bare and caked with grime. He was staring at Puss so intensely that Puss had to look away. Puss turned back a few seconds later. The prisoner was still staring, just as hard.

"Looks like the egg got what he wanted," he said.

Puss frowned. "You're talking about Humpty Du—"

"Don't say his name!" snarled the old man. "I used to share this cell with that smelly thing. Happiest day of my life was when he left, until I realized he stole my magic beans."

"Wait, wait, wait! You had the beans?" Puss asked. That didn't make any sense at all.

"He snatched 'em when I was asleep," said the old man. "I should have seen it coming." The prisoner sighed as a great sadness seemed to fall over him, but then moments later, he was sound asleep and snoring loudly.

"Wake up!" Puss yelled. "What else do you know?"

"The prisoner startled awake. "I know a secret," he said mysteriously before falling right back asleep.

"What secret?" Puss yelled again, slapping the prisoner to try to wake him up.

The prisoner, awake again, if only for a moment, replied, "The Great Terror is the Golden Goose's mama! And that egg won't be such a hero when she comes back here for her baby."

Puss sprang to his feet and ran to the prison cell door. "Guard!" he hollered through the bars. "San Ricardo is in terrible danger. You must listen to me!"

"Quiet, you!" the guard barked back, covering his ears. Who wanted to listen to a crazy, disgraced outlaw? He had nothing to say that they wanted to hear.

CHAPTER
THIRTEEN

Puss paced. If only he could break out of his cell. Then he could warn the villagers and save the town! But how? It was clear that no one would ever believe a word that came out of his mouth now.

Exactly how long did they have, he wondered, until the Great Terror arrived?

A few minutes later, the prison guard heard another sound coming from the cell, but it wasn't Puss's pleas. It sounded more like high-pitched shrieks. Annoyed, the guard marched up to Puss's cell to tell him to shut up. But when he peered through the bars he didn't say a word because he was suddenly struck dumb.

Puss stood, staring at him with his biggest, most hypnotic eyes.

"Open the door," he commanded and, entranced, the guard obeyed.

"Drop the weapon," Puss went on in the same low, firm tone.

The guard dropped his sword.

"Very good. Step aside," ordered Puss.

The guard took a step back, then seemed to remember suddenly who he was and where. "No . . . devil cat!" he cried, snapping out of his trance-like state. He held up a squirt bottle and sprayed Puss with water.

"Nice try," the guard scoffed as Puss shrank back, shaking the droplets from his nose. Then the next thing he knew, two soft paws covered the man's face and pulled him to the ground.

Kitty stepped into the light to Puss's astonishment. "I hope you can forgive me," she said.

"Apology accepted!" yelped the old prisoner, running past Puss, whooping and hollering to be free from his chains at last.

Puss just stood there, however, glaring at Kitty. "You knew. All along you knew and said nothing," he growled.

He stormed past finally, but Kitty followed him. "Please listen to me," she begged. "There's a way out, but you have to trust me."

"And why should I trust you?" he asked. For all Puss knew, Kitty was still working with the dirty, rotten egg.

Kitty held up her paw. "Because you're the first cat I've met who gives me hope," she replied. "And that's something I lost a long time ago. Please, Ginger, I owe this to you."

Just then an alarm bell rang and the two cats looked up. "They're down here!" a guard yelled.

Kitty quickly handed Puss his hat, cape, sword and boots, which she had lifted from the Comandante's safe. He took them and looked deep into her apologetic cobalt eyes. They seemed to say, without a doubt, *You can trust me.*

"Go, Puss, run!" Kitty urged.

"No more running. I won't leave San Ricardo

in danger," Puss replied. He wasn't going to let the village down again.

"OK, I'll hold them off," Kitty told him.

"Hurry!" another guard was calling.

Puss smiled gratefully and slipped his boots on, then tossed on his cape and cap and grabbed his sword. He sprinted down the hall. "I am still mad at you!" he called, looking over his shoulder.

The Comandante, meanwhile, had ordered every prison guard to chase down Puss.

"There he is!" he shouted at the sight of a cat in a hooded cape and boots fleeing through a window out onto the roof. "Cut him off!" he commanded, sending his soldiers off in two groups.

They followed the cat as it scampered along the rooftops, determined to corner it, and they did. No sooner had the cat leaped onto a balcony, than they surrounded it.

"You are not getting away this time, Puss In Boots!" the Comandante declared. He grinned as the cat turned around and slowly pulled his hood back. Then he quickly frowned to discover that the cat they had cornered wasn't Puss In Boots after all.

"Wrong boots," Kitty said coyly, smiling down at the dainty brown heels on her feet.

At the same time, Humpty was at the centre of a celebratory parade in the town square. Villagers danced in the streets, clutching golden eggs. Humpty, perched on top of a float, threw more golden eggs to the cheering crowd.

Puss suddenly flew through the air and caught one of the eggs. All the villagers gasped and the parade ground to a halt.

"Everyone! Drop the eggs! Get off the streets!" Puss yelled wildly, trying to warn the villagers.

"Don't listen to him!" Humpty called as he struggled to get down from the float. Turning to Puss, Humpty continued, "You just can't handle that this is my moment to be the hero!"

"This isn't about you or me." If only Humpty would understand! "It's about saving these people . . ." But Puss's voice was drowned out by a loud, screeching roar as the Great Terror plummeted down from the sky towards San

Ricardo. The sky grew dark. Terror would strike San Ricardo in moments.

"What is that?" Humpty shouted.

"That is the Great Terror!" Puss shouted back. "The Great Terror is the Golden Goose's mama!"

Humpty's face filled with horror and realization. "This can't be the legend . . ." he mumbled.

"Just get the baby across the bridge," Puss instructed. "I will lead the mama to you!"

Humpty just stared at Puss. "Are you crazy? These things bite! We have to get out of here!"

"This is your fault!" Puss reminded Humpty. "You wanted to be the hero of San Ricardo. Now is your chance! Recite the Bean Club oath!"

Humpty turned to his friend and said "Never alone . . . always together?"

"We will do this together," Puss replied, looking Humpty in the eye. "You owe me this much."

The Great Terror set down and screams began to fill the village streets. With a furious *"HISSSSS!"*

the Mother Goose swooped down and planted her giant webbed feet in the center of town. As they watched the chaos, Puss turned to Humpty and repeated, "Get the baby over the bridge! I'll get the mother to follow!"

And so Humpty grabbed the Golden Goose and did as Puss said.

Meanwhile, Puss saw a chance to subdue Mother Goose and leaped onto her back, hand-springing up till he reached her neck. Then he used the string of a banner stretched across one face of the bell tower to harness the creature's beak and head. "Come with me, Mama Goose! I know where your baby is!" With that, he steered her huge head toward the road out of town.

At that moment, Humpty's cart was rolling down that road, and the Golden Goose was sitting in the back of that cart. The goose honked at its mother and she happily honked back.

The Great Terror started to chase the cart down. According to plan, Puss almost had her safely out of town before she could do any more damage.

CHAPTER

FOURTEEN

"Humpty, pick up the pace!" Puss called from his perch on the Great Terror's neck.

The egg's cart hadn't yet reached the bridge, and the Mother Goose had nearly caught up. So far, Puss's plan was working, but he still had to get the beast *out* of San Ricardo.

"I'm trying, Puss, I'm trying!" the egg yelled. He snapped the reins harder. "Please go faster!" he begged.

Then who should cross the road in front of him just then but the Comandante's elderly mum. There was no way she could jump out of his way. Humpty was going to run her over for sure this time! Desperate, the egg grabbed for the lever on the side of his cart and frantically pulled it back. And it worked! The wings released just in time, and the cart sailed over the old woman, missing her by a gray hair.

"Almost there. We're almost there!" shouted Humpty as he flew towards the bridge. But he hadn't counted on the wings being too wide for the bridge tower. They clipped the stone arch and the wagon careened.

BAM!

The cart hit the side of the bridge and instantly tumbled out of control. Out flew both Humpty and the Golden Goose. They slammed into the Mother Goose, flinging Puss off her neck and onto the bridge, which soon began to crumble from her weight. The beast wailed and fell to the river below, as more of the bridge collapsed on top of her.

The whole bridge was falling and there was no stopping it! Humpty rolled towards the edge. "Puss, help!" he cried.

"Humpty, hang on!" Puss called as he raced to

help. But he was too late. *"Puss!"* Humpty rolled off the side and disappeared.

Puss didn't give up, though. He lunged and just barely caught the leash that Humpty was still holding, saving both Humpty and the Golden Goose at once. Still, the two were heavy for just one Puss, and it was all he could do to hold on. Far below, the Mother Goose writhed beneath the bridge rubble, making it crumble even more.

Humpty gazed up at Puss as he dangled helplessly above the boulder-filled gorge. "Here we are again, right, Puss?" he gulped. On the bridge . . . like the time Puss had left him, declaring, "No more."

Puss looked the egg hard in the eye. "I will not leave you behind this time, Humpty," he swore.

He tightened his grip on the leash, but his muscles were getting weak. "Pull yourself up!" Puss urged Humpty as more and more of the bridge fell away.

But Humpty couldn't. His skinny limbs weren't made to hoist so much body weight.

He looked over at the Golden Goose, who was slipping from Puss's grip as well. "You can't save us both," he said.

"Yes, I can! Just hang on!" Puss said, determined.

"Puss, you have to get the goose back to its mother. You know it's the only way to save San Ricardo."

"No, Humpty. I can do it," Puss bravely assured him.

But beneath Puss's fur Humpty could see his muscles tremble, and the strain was plain in Puss's face. "I won't make you choose. That much I owe you," the egg told his friend. And with that, Humpty closed his eyes one last time and let go of the leash.

"Humpty!" Puss cried as he reached out desperately. He felt something and grabbed it. The leash! He pulled up.

The Golden Goose was safe.

There wasn't much left of the bridge when the Mother Goose finally freed herself from the rubble. But the town of San Ricardo was saved.

Puss returned the Golden Goose to her, saying, "I'm very sorry. She's OK."

But his old friend, alas, was not. He lay on a boulder beside the river unconscious. Puss hung his head in mourning. He had finally restored a lost friendship . . . only to lose it all over again.

The egg's shell was covered with cracks, but as Puss watched, amazed, from above, it slowly began to peel away. Like the petals of a flower, in fact, it unfolded gently to reveal something truly remarkable: a perfect egg-shaped body made entirely out of gold!

Humpty's eyes fluttered opened and he smiled up at Puss. "Oh, Puss, I'm gold! Look, look, look, look, look! Even my teeth are gold."

The cat wiped away a happy tear. "I always knew," said Puss.

And with that, the Mother Goose plopped her golden gosling on her neck, then flapped her giant wings and took off. She made a graceful arc before swooping back down and plucking up the now golden Humpty. As the three of them sailed off toward the setting sun, Humpty dreamily said: "I'm finally going home."

Puss saluted the happy family. "Goodbye, Humpty," he called.

"Who is that?" Imelda turned at the sound of footsteps in the dusty yard behind the orphanage.

Almost like a ghost, Puss stepped out of the early evening shadows. "It is me, Mama. I am sorry," he said. "I never wanted to disappoint you."

The old woman rushed forward, her arms open, and wrapped Puss in a warm hug. "There is nothing to forgive," she whispered.

Puss felt a warm blanket of relief enfold him. "But I am still an outlaw," he murmured.

Imelda released him and gripped his shoulders. "Not to me," she said with a proud smile. "Today you faced the past with bravery and honour. You earned those boots. Always stay true to them, *Pequeño*."

Puss hugged her once more and kissed her. "Anything for you, Mama," he said.

"You will always be in my heart," she told him. "Now be a good boy. Not too much messing around with the girls, OK?"

Puss blushed beneath his furry stripes. Then a guard's voice pierced the peaceful night. *"Freeze!"*

But the guard was too late to catch Puss In Boots. He slipped into the shadows once more and soon waved to Imelda from a roof, far away.

Of course, there was still someone else Puss needed to say goodbye to . . . and he found her making her way along the rooftops, as well.

"I will see you again, Kitty Softpaws," Puss purred as they raced along, dodging guards and dancing, matching each other move for more.

Kitty's smiled, her eyes sparkling like bright blue diamonds. "Sooner than you think."

Then she bounded away, across the rooftops, and Puss sighed as he watched her go. There was definitely something special about that cat . . .

Then he frowned. Wait. Something was wrong.

He looked down. His *boots*. They were gone!

When he looked back up, he saw Kitty in the distance, waving his boots above her head.

"Oh, she is a bad kitty," he said with a grin. Just the kind he liked best!

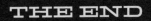

THE END